SECOND CHANCE FOR LOVE

Second Chance Regency Romance (Book 2)

ROSE PEARSON

SECOND CHANCE
FOR LOVE

PROLOGUE

Grover House, Tynson, Leicestershire, 1814

"Mary? Mary? Must I hunt you down?" The harsh crackle of Jane Grover's voice resonated throughout the small house. Mary was sure the neighbors could hear it, but it would have been an accustomed sound. She couldn't remember a single instance when Aunt Jane had spoken to her kindly.

"Yes, Aunt?" Mary said, hurrying to the parlor, where her aunt stood with her eyes narrowed and her cheeks flushed with annoyance.

"What is this? You call this clean?" Aunt Jane pointed her long finger at the oak dresser, its counter still marked with stains.

"I have done the best I could, Aunt," Mary tried to explain. "But there is no getting the stains out. I told Roberta not to use the dyes in here, to take them into the workshop, as you have always directed - but she wouldn't listen. She insisted it was too cold there, and that she wouldn't work away from the fire."

"Don't blame my daughter for your incompetence," her aunt snapped. "Where she tests our dyes and does her work is not your business. She is a part of this family's trade. She works hard and earns her keep - unlike you, who costs me an arm and a leg to feed." She gave Mary a hard look and sighed dramatically. "If I had known your father would be gone so long, and we would have to take care of you for nine, long years when we took you in, I would never have done it. I should have thought twice of it, knowing how feckless and useless your father has always been, his head in the clouds with his stupid inventions."

"My father is a good man," Mary protested. "He will come back. And he will have made his fortune, I know it," Mary said willing herself to keep believing it, though she'd not had so much as a single letter from him in two years, since he'd written to tell her he was headed for America, two years earlier, in the hope of finding a buyer for his newest invention. "He promised," she whispered to herself.

Aunt Jane scoffed. "And we both believed him, more fool us," she said. "But that is by-the-by. Get this cleaned." She clouted Mary around the head without so much as a flicker of warning. Mary staggered under the force of the blow but knew better than to whimper or complain. "The vicar will be stopping by this afternoon for tea," Aunt Jane continued as if she'd not just made Mary's ears ring. "I shall not be able to receive him if you cannot do your work properly."

Mary said nothing further as her aunt stalked from the room. There was no use in doing so. The story was always the same. Aunt Jane was a saint for taking her in, and Mary was an expense the family could ill-afford. Nobody seemed to notice that Mary herself had been given no choice in the matter, or that she worked her fingers to the bone to keep the house clean and keep the entire family fed.

The Grover's were not wealthy people. They made what little coin they could from their business making and selling dyes to the local cloth mills. In truth, they had benefitted from Mary's arrival. It had saved them the cost of keeping a maid and a cook, as Mary had been put to work the moment her father had left for London. He'd sent money, from time to time, but Mary had seen nothing of it. She made her clothes from the hand-me-downs of her cousin Roberta and had only two gowns – one for work, and one for church. Both were worn thin from washing and she did her best to keep them smart, though neither was truly fit for wearing.

With a heavy sigh, Mary went to fetch the bucket and scrubbing brushes from the scullery. Rolled up neatly, and pressed into the corner out of the way, was her bed. Constructed from old sheets and rags that Aunt Jane had consigned to be used for cleaning, Mary had done what she could to make it comfortable, to save her from sleeping directly upon the bare flagstones. It was cold in the tiny scullery, with no heating, save that which came through from the kitchen next door, and Mary had barely had a warm night in all her time in the Grover household, even in the height of summer.

Her thoughts raced as she went into the yard and filled the bucket from the well, then went to the kitchen to fetch a bar of soap. Mary knew the truth, even if her father had not chosen to be aware of it when he left her with his sister-in-law and her husband. The Grovers hated her. They hated Papa more, but his money was something they would gladly take for themselves when it came – even as they derided him for his pie-in-the-sky dreams.

Aunt Jane had never approved of the match between Papa and Mama. She had always sneered at his inventions and had chastised him for not taking a proper position once he had a wife to support, and their criticisms had only grown once Mary had been born. In their eyes, it was all his fault that Mama had passed away, from illness, ten years ago now.

Mary knew none of their complaints of him were true, and she held fast to that knowledge in the darkness, as she prayed every night for his return. Despite all the work that Papa had put into his inventions, as a family they had never suffered. They had been blessed with a roof over their head. True, it had been the smallest of cottages, but it had been clean and well-kept. They had been clothed in good quality fabrics, warm woolens and soft cottons, though they had made all their clothes themselves. And there had been fresh food upon the table, in sufficient quantities to nourish them all - unlike here, where she ate the scraps from her aunt's table and had become thin and gaunt.

Wearily, Mary made her way back upstairs to the parlor and began to scrub at the dresser. Aunt Jane had an iron will and a quick temper. All too often Mary had felt the sting of the rod on her back for her failures to achieve the impossible. Uncle William had never laid a hand on her. To tell the truth, Mary wondered if he ever even deigned to notice she was there as he never did anything to stop the punishments, or to even acknowledge her with so much as a nod. But it was not Uncle William that wielded the power in this household. Aunt Jane was lord and master here, and her children after her.

As she scrubbed as hard as she could, Mary recalled the icy cold feeling that had filled the house as soon as

Papa had gone, all those years ago. She had been just ten years old and had still been mourning the loss of her beloved Mama. But Papa had insisted he would only be gone for a few months at most, that he would find someone in London who would believe in his inventions and that he would return for her.

Mary had sobbed as he hugged her goodbye and Aunt Jane had assured Papa that she would take good care of little Mary. Yet, as soon as the door had closed behind him, her aunt's demeanor had changed completely. Aunt Jane had scoffed at Mary, ridiculing her speech for being too la-di-da - and when she discovered Mary could read a little, while her children could not, Aunt Jane's barbs had become ever sharper.

Mary could not understand why Aunt Jane would accuse her of thinking herself better than them, as she thought no such thing. It was not her fault that Papa had wanted the best for her and had done what he could to provide her with an excellent education. Not that anyone would know it now. Anything she had learned as a child before she came to live in her aunt's house, had long since departed. She was more ignorant now than she had been as a child of ten.

She wiped away the soap suds and frowned. The stains from the indigo dye were not shifting. Mary knew well enough that the only way to truly remove them would be to sand down the surface of the dresser – but she knew her aunt would not hear of that. She sighed and started to scrub again.

The sound of raucous laughter filtered through the open window. Mary looked up as the door of the house was flung open loudly, and her cousin, Felix, staggered inside. Mary hurried to the hallway. The stench of alcohol filled the air of the dark and un-aired space. He stumbled towards her. Mary tried to get out of his way, but he seemed intent on making it impossible.

"Out of my way, wench," he demanded as he grabbed her roughly by the arms and tossed her aside. Mary fell to the floor with a thud, her back colliding with the heavy oak post at the bottom of the stairwell. Felix, unstable on his legs, held on to the newel post and glared at Mary coldly as she lay gasping at the pain, trying to catch her breath. "Get me something to eat," he demanded.

Mary pulled herself to her feet and went to the empty kitchen to fetch him bread and cheese. Felix was a terrible drunk – and he seemed to be drunk more often than he was sober. His life was not as he wanted; he hated his work in the dye works and the power his mother still wielded over him - and he believed drink would remedy his problems. It never did, as Aunt Jane would never have permitted him to have a thought of his own, much less act on them.

And so, he was as unhappy as Mary. The only difference was, he had Mary to lash out at, to express his impotent fury. Perhaps she might have had more sympathy for his miserable life if he'd been more sympathetic to her plight – but he always kicked down, and only added to her woes with his spite. Still, Mary did as she was told and tried to please him – as she did everyone, in the hope that perhaps things might change one day.

She handed her cousin the plate of food. He looked at the plain fare and threw it across the room, the pewter plate clattering loudly on the uneven flagstones. Mary braced herself for his tirade, but instead, they both turned at the sound of Aunt Jane's heavy tread on the stairs. "What is all this commotion?" she demanded as she came towards them, then saw the swaying form of her son and the discarded bread and cheese on the floor. She frowned.

Felix looked up at his mother, as Mary stood silently by. His bravado disappeared and a look of fear crossed his face. "Mary has caused a mess, Mother," he simpered. "I told her to get me something to eat - and she tossed the plate at me."

"Did she, indeed?" Aunt Jane said, her tone icy cold. She turned to Mary. "You threw food at my son?"

Mary clenched her teeth, the desire to defend herself sharp on her tongue, but wisdom told her to remain silent. She had already had one run-in too many with her aunt this day, another would not end any better. Aunt Jane would never hear the truth. Mary lowered her eyes and prayed that her aunt's anger would be soon spent.

In moments, Aunt Jane was stood in front of her. "Answer me," she demanded as she slapped Mary's cheek, making Mary's head snap to the right. Her cheek stung and her eye throbbed as if it might explode.

Mary grabbed her cheek, tears stinging her eyes. "I am terribly sorry, Aunt Jane. I meant no trouble."

"You never mean trouble, but that is all you ever cause," Aunt Jane said angrily. "Now, go and fetch Felix something substantial to eat. There is beef in the pantry leftover from last night's roast, some pickles perhaps, and some fresh bread. Then get out of my sight. There will be no food for you tonight."

Mary nodded and bit her tongue. Protesting the unfairness of any punishment would do her no good. It was not the first time she would go to bed hungry, and it was unlikely that it would be the last. Her stomach no longer bothered to protest the emptiness, it happened so often. But as she prepared the meal for her cousin, the injustice festered more strongly than before. She would not take this any longer. It was time for her to act, to take care of herself – as nobody else would.

Hours passed and the house creaked, every sound making Mary's heart race faster. She heard the vicar come and go, and the family served themselves a cold supper before retiring to bed. Mary waited in the scullery, out of sight, as she had been told, planning her escape, until the house was as quiet as it ever was.

There was no clock to tell the time by, only the increasing cold seeping through the cracked timbers of the draughty house. She shivered, pulling her thin shawl tighter around her shoulders, and looked at the meager pile of items she intended to take with her. She had little to her name and wanted nothing from those she would leave behind.

She wrapped up a hunk of bread and a piece of cheese in a muslin cloth, packed the bible that Mama had given her and the small silver cross that her father had pressed into her hand the day he'd left, and bundled them into a basket. In truth, much as she would preserve these precious mementos, she only needed one thing, to find her father, even if that meant traveling all the way to America, alone.

She jimmied the floorboard below her bedroll and reached inside, pulling out a small purse, containing the few coins she'd managed to save that Papa had given directly to her when he left her with her aunt, as a child. She peeked inside, relieved that nobody had ever found her hiding spot. If they had, she had no doubt that the money would have been taken and spent on her cousins. She knew it was unlikely that it was enough to get her to America, but it may perhaps get her as far as London, where she might be able to barter her skills as a housemaid in return for her passage.

She had oft thought of running away but never dared to do so. She had continued to hope that Papa would someday come for her. But she could no longer take the neglect and solitude of her aunt and uncle's home. Nine years had felt like an eternity, and things had only gotten worse since Papa had written to tell them of his intention to go to America. They'd not heard anything from him since, and her aunt had taken that as an invitation to heap ever more cruelties upon Mary's thin shoulders.

The silence was heavy around her, and Mary's skin prickled as she crept towards the door. She stopped, her hand upon the latch, as a loud creak above her head shattered the silence. Her breath caught in her lungs as she searched for a source of the noise, waiting for it to repeat. It did not. She pulled the door open, her feet hesitant on the threshold.

Could she truly do this?

Her father had wanted her to stay here. He had bid her be good for her aunt and had made all those promises to her. He had been so sure that her aunt would care for her - but Papa did not know what Mary had been forced to endure for the pleasure of the roof over her head. She was sure he would not have wanted her to stay if he had known. He was a sweet and good man. He would not have thought such cruelty possible.

Mary closed the door quietly behind her and stood in the street, the ground mucky from the frequent rains of the past weeks. She looked down at her boots. They were worn and full of holes. They were barely fit for working in the house and would not hold up to the rigors of traveling, but they were all she had.

Tynson was small, barely a scratch of a town. It had but one coaching inn. Mary made her way along the High Street and was glad to see that, despite the late hour, there were still lights blazing from the windows. Coaches sat ready for departure outside. She hurried forward, excited and afraid of what her future would hold, glad to finally be one of the passengers to leave this place.

Without looking where she was going, in her haste, she stepped into a puddle. The dirty water seeped through the holes in the soles of her boots, soaking her woolen stockings, making her shiver even more. Wishing she'd had the foresight to at least take one of Roberta's winter coats and an additional pair of socks, Mary kicked her legs to try to get some of the water out before proceeding, though she knew it was futile.

A coach stood outside the inn, the horse's breath billowing in the cold night air. The driver was cloaked in black, with a top hat on his head, and wore a heavy coat, woolen muffler, and sheepskin mittens. He perched on the bench and pulled off one of his mittens to light the lamps, then put it back on swiftly.

"Sir?" Mary called to him when she was close. "How much is the fare to London?"

"That's about a hundred miles, Miss," he said thoughtfully. "I can take you there for three crowns, three shillins, miss – if you take your seat up on the bench with me," he replied. "If'n you want a seat inside, and on a night like this, it'd be best – and I'd get you a hot brick from the inn and a blanket, too - well that'd be one pound and three crowns."

Mary gasped as she looked at the five shillings in her purse. She knew that travel wasn't cheap but had not expected it to be so very expensive. "How far can I get for five shillings?" she asked anxiously.

"That'll get you thirty miles, young miss, up here on the box with me - about as far as Alnerton," the man replied. "If you want to go then you need to decide now, I am leaving shortly."

There was no going back. If Alnerton was as far she could go by coach, then she would walk the rest of the way, though seventy miles sounded an awfully long distance to go on foot. She offered the coin to him. "Passage for one to Alnerton, on the box."

He gave her a gentle smile, checked the trunks on the roof were fixed securely, then got down and went into the inn. Mary heard him holler out to his passengers that he was leaving, and a number of well-clad men and women traipsed out into the cold behind him. He opened the door and let them inside, then offered Mary his hand up onto the bench.

She scrambled up and settled herself, her teeth chattering loudly as he jumped up beside her. He reached into a box beneath the bench and pulled out a thick blanket. "Wrap yourself up, little one," he said kindly. Mary took it and wrapped it around herself tightly, forcing her fear and concern aside. She would be fine. She would get to her destination safely.

She fell asleep along the way, her head nodding onto the shoulder of the coachman. Despite the cold, she only roused when a firm hand gripped her shoulder. "Your stop," her kindly coachman told her.

Mary looked up at the rolling fields before her. There was no sign of life anywhere. "Here?"

"This is the stop for Alnerton," he assured her. "At least as close as I go. You walk that way a few miles," he nodded to a lane that went off to their left, "and you will reach Alnerton itself. If you carry on along this road, it'll take you to London - eventually."

Mary turned to look at both options. Both looked dark and desolate. She felt a stab of panic as she thought of the perils that lay in the darkness for an unaccompanied traveler. She turned to ask him how long he thought it might take her to get to London, but he had already clicked his tongue and the coach had moved away, leaving Mary to decide her next step, alone.

The dawn was starting to break, the sky lightening as the sun crept up above the horizon, and there was mist hovering in patches along the lanes. Mary was torn. Should she go to the town? It was closer, and the road seemed less frightening, but doing so would take her further away from her destination, and she had no money for lodgings or even a loaf of bread when she got there.

There was no real choice. She had to continue onwards. Every step would take her closer to London, and closer to her father. She could not afford to waste time or energy on anything else. She turned to the road to London and, hooking her basket over her arm and forcing herself to sing a merry tune, she began to walk.

She walked for hours. Dawn arrived with a heavy grey cloud that seemed to be following her. She sped up, hoping she might be able to get to some shelter before it reached her, but there was nowhere. The storm came with a loud crash of thunder and rain pelted down on her. It was icy cold, and she was soon drenched to the skin and shaking uncontrollably, but she had to go on.

She'd barely covered ten miles, that first day. Her feet were covered in blisters from her ill-fitting boots, her legs wobbled. Her body was weak from lack of food and the bitter cold, but she gritted her teeth and kept on trudging as night began to fall and she started to fear she might not find somewhere to shelter for the night.

She was so caught up in her thoughts, and the sound of the pouring rain, that Mary barely heard the hoofbeats approaching her from behind. But as she stumbled and briefly looked behind to see what had prompted her fall, she saw the light of a coach approach. Relieved and elated, she staggered into the middle of the road to get the driver's attention. Perhaps they would show pity on her and take her to the closest shelter.

The horses were running fast, and Mary feared they might not see her, and might knock her down. She mustered her courage and stood her ground but panicked when the coach drew near with no sign of stopping. She threw herself into the tall grass of the verge, out of harm's way. She felt her ankle twist beneath her and cried out in pain. She tried to raise a hand and call for help, but she did not have the strength. Her entire body felt heavy. Mary closed her eyes, giving in to the exhaustion she felt in every inch of her body. She only hoped they would open again.

CHAPTER ONE

L ondon, 1818

A jovial tune was playing in the parlor of Merrick House. William Pierce, the Eighth Earl Cott, heir to the Duchy of Mormont, stood with a glass of wine in hand and smiled enthusiastically at the charming young lady before him. She was possessed of red hair, brown eyes, and a large gap between her teeth that he found surprisingly pleasant. Her name was Belinda Nolan and rumor had it that she had an income of ten thousand pounds a year. Given such knowledge, it was not unsurprising that she was one of the most popular debutantes present this Season.

"Miss Nolan, it is a pleasure to meet you." William bowed his head politely.

The young woman smiled, fluttering her eyelashes at him. "The pleasure is all mine, my Lord."

"Did I not tell you that London has its charms?" Claveston St. John, Fourth Earl of Wycliffe chuckled, as he came up behind William as Miss Nolan moved away to join her friends, her comely figure swaying enticingly.

William had attended school with Wycliffe, and his old friend had extended a welcome invitation to join him and his family in London for the Season. William didn't much enjoy Society, preferring to keep to himself in the country as much as possible. Alnerton was his home, and he was happiest there, with his sister and her husband. But being at Alnerton also meant being under his father's eye, and William, weary from the Duke's constant criticisms, had decided to accept the invitation to join his friend for a few weeks.

William sipped his wine. "Yes, you did," he admitted, with a soft chuckle.

"Then why did it take so much to convince you to come?" Claveston said with a grin. "You cannot tell me that Alnerton has anything on London."

"Wycliffe, we cannot all run around the country indulging our whims. Some of us have serious business to attend to," William replied with a grin, teasing his reckless friend just a little.

Claveston scoffed. "Serious business? As if your father would ever permit you to do anything of import."

William had to admit that Claveston was right. His father was the type of man that had to manage every single detail himself. For a duke, William's father was unusually involved in the running of not just the family estate, but also their many investments. Whereas most members of the aristocracy would hire overseers and managers to run things for them, never soiling their hands with anything so tawdry as work, the Duke of Mormont would not hear of it. He was convinced that such matters should be private – and that anyone else was not to be trusted with the family's affairs.

Claveston looked unusually put out at the implication that William did not think him serious. "I have matters to deal with," he protested, "just because they do not restrict me to one town does not make them any less important. Our family's interests require close investigation, and my father trusts me to undertake matters on his behalf, it extends his reach."

"Unlike mine," William said wryly. "I doubt he'd trust me to so much as choose my own horse." He took a large mouthful of his wine, draining the glass dry. "And when does your father set off again on his travels?"

"In a fortnight, perhaps three weeks," Claveston replied. "He intends to travel to America, with his newest business associate to take care of some matters of import there, then he travels to Lisbon, Spain, and Majorca. He will be gone for six months, at least. I must remain here in London, whilst he is gone to oversee his interests here. I will return to Compton upon his return."

"How convenient for you, that his travels should coincide with the Season," William said with a grin. Claveston enjoyed Society life and would not find being in London for such a long period of time any kind of hardship.

"You know me too well, my friend. It is nice to have a distraction from the day-to-day troubles I shall have to take responsibility for."

William shook his head. Though very different in their approaches, the Duke of Compton and his own father were unusually active in matters of business – but while William's father insisted on overseeing every tiny element, Claveston's father was much more of a figurehead – as would be expected. He had connections in every industry, from finance to imports, and traveled the world to visit his many investments - yet never soiled his hands with actually doing a day's work. Though Claveston would no doubt be kept busy, William knew that none of his tasks would be as onerous as he made out.

William was sure that the difference in approach of the two dukes was the reason why the Compton fortune so exceeded that of the House of Mormont. His own father would only ever invest in things he could be directly involved in, that he could manage and keep under his eye. A far-flung empire was not something the Duke of Mormont could ever countenance, as it would mean trusting others with his affairs.

"Of course, he has excellent men in place to oversee his many investments," Claveston continued. "But he must check on everything himself. Even the matters I handle whilst he is away, he will follow up on when he returns. Everything must be perfect."

William patted his friend's arm. He knew the pressures of constant supervision; it was a burden that he and Claveston shared, though the Duke of Compton was not ever-present like his own father seemed to be. "Do not worry," he assured his friend. "We are here now, and there is plenty to amuse us. Let us put aside our fathers and business for the evening, and you may continue to introduce me to London society."

"Gladly," Claveston said, clapping William on the back. "There are some ladies that I would like you to meet. They are friends of Miss Maria and the Comtesse Paulina, the ladies we met in Portugal, during our Grand Tour. Do you remember?"

"I certainly do," William said, smiling at the memories of their wonderful time on the Continent. "The Comtesse believed herself in love with me. She practically had our wedding set and our children named," William chuckled. "Did I ever thank you for rescuing me?"

"Many times," Claveston replied. "But I never grow tired of hearing it."

William laughed. It was good to be away from his father and the constant pressures put upon him. Since Charlotte had left the house upon her marriage to James Watts, Caldor House was once again without mirth. Though Charlotte was only a few miles away, she had her commitments to her own family to think of first.

As he followed Claveston, William thought he saw a familiar face across the room. He squinted, trying to get a better look amidst the ocean of faces. It seemed his old friend had invited half of London to the party, and one could hardly find a free space from one end of the room to another. He tried to pay attention to the young lady that Claveston thrust before him, but again a glimpse of dark blonde curls caught his eye, this time, with a face he was sure he knew.

It could not be. Could it?

William tried not to be obvious as he leaned closer to his friend. "Wycliffe, that young lady over there. Who is she?"

His friend laughed. "Which? There are so many."

"Over there," William pointed as discretely as he could. "The young woman in white muslin, blonde curls - standing near the lady in the emerald dress with the feather in her hair," William elaborated.

"Oh, her," Claveston said a little dismissively. "Her name is Miss Mary Durand. My father has invested in some invention of her father's. He created a process, canning, that Father thinks will change everything in food transportation. Peter Durand sold the patent in America, and his partner there put him in touch with my father. He's become rather wealthy from it all. Father has asked me to ensure that his daughter finds a place in Society."

So, it was her. William would hardly believe it was the same young woman he nursed back to health some three years before. There was no trace of the frail girl, whose health had caused him such alarm when he found her half-dead along the roadside. Instead, a beautiful woman, full-cheeked and bright-smiled, stood in her place – though her eyes darted nervously about the room, still filled with the same anxiety he remembered.

William wanted to go to her, to find out what had happened after she returned to her father's house. They had lost touch, despite his desire to remain close by. She was an admirable young woman to have endured the things she had and still find a way to smile. And it was her smile that had always delighted him most. Warm and sincere, whenever she had cast it in his direction, he had felt a stirring deep inside him. He wondered if it would be the same now. He was eager to find out.

"William? Are you listening?" Claveston's voice shattered his thoughts and brought him back to earth. The young ladies Claveston had been introducing him to were looking at him strangely, no doubt wondering where his mind had gone.

"Forgive me, I was momentarily distracted," William apologized.

"I can see that." Claveston once again looked in Mary's direction. "Do you know her?"

William could not hide the smile that broke across his face as he answered. "I do, though it has been many years since we last saw each other."

"Truly?" The young brunette who stood before him inquired. "You know such a person?"

The tone of her voice was not lost on him. It dripped with disdain and William wondered why. "Do you know her?"

The young woman scoffed. "Certainly not. I would never be associated with the likes of her. My father is the Viscount of Brodney. He would disown me should I bring home anyone in trade."

William bristled as a ripple of laughter spread amongst the party. "A goodly number of the aristocracy is wed to the daughters of merchants," he pointed out tartly.

"And that is to their shame," the young woman said spitefully. "She has no name, and her presence is only borne because of her seven thousand pounds a year." She turned to Claveston. "Your father would do well to be wary of that."

"My father considers everything," his friend replied, grinning, clearly not bothered by the woman's malice, or that a woman whose father's rank was below his own was attempting to tell him how to behave.

William looked at him silently. "Does he?"

"Of course," his friend replied. "My father would not be the man he is, if he did not."

"The lady is not a matter of business, and your father expects you to introduce her to society. Is this how you do it? By letting others speak ill of her?"

Claveston's jovial expression disappeared, replaced by a look of discomfort. He lowered his voice to speak. "Cott, I will handle it, but now is not the time. She will do well enough on her own, and later, when the time is right, I will introduce her properly."

William was aghast. Was the influence of his guests so

great that he would slight Mary for them? He did not know her, or her story. If they did, maybe they would understand, as he did. "Surely, the time to let the world know she has the patronage of the son of the Duke of Compton, would be the moment she appears in your home?"

"She is of low birth. Why bother?" the young lady who had already besmirched Mary's name so badly said with a snigger.

William had never been more glad that he had not paid attention when introduced to this unfeeling creature. It would make it far easier to forget her, though her unkindness would be harder to dismiss. "Low birth?" William countered sharply, his temper rising.

Claveston looked at him curiously. "How did you come to meet this young lady? You have never mentioned her to me before?"

All eyes were upon him, and William couldn't help but feel uncomfortable, but he knew that his discomfort must feel like a mere inconvenience when compared to the disdain and spite Mary was being subjected to. William turned in Mary's direction. She had retreated into a corner, her smile had faded and she was fidgeting with her gown, her shoulders hunched as if she wished the ground might swallow her whole.

The young woman laughed spitefully. "As Earl Cott, heir to the Duchy of Mormont, why would he mention meeting someone like her? Whatever acquaintance they had it could hardly be worth remembering. Perhaps an encounter in the market where her father was packing fish? She wrapped some trout for him."

"Whatever my acquaintance with Miss Durand, I assure you, it is none of your concern," William said through clenched teeth. He was barely containing his temper, though he knew the mores of Society required that he must.

The young woman, sensing his building anger, turned to her companion. "Come, Hortense," she said. "I see the Duchess of Aberdeen. I should go and pay my respects. Her Grace was most complimentary about my gown at Almack's last week."

The young women departed swiftly. William was glad to see them go. If they saw Mary in such a light, a woman he considered a friend, they could never be an acquaintance of his. But Claveston was not so discerning, or so it would seem.

"Ladies," he pleaded. "Please do not go." He hurried after them. "My friend takes things to heart. Please, forgive him."

When they continued to move away, Claveston turned back to William. "Look at what you have done," he hissed." I am trying to introduce you to London Society and you offend two of the most eligible ladies here this Season. Was that necessary?"

William looked at his friend, wondering if he knew him at all. "Were their words necessary?" he asked Wycliffe. "They spoke of Miss Durand as if they had some idea of her when they had none. They slandered her good character."

Claveston frowned, his voice still a whisper. "They said nothing you would not have heard before. I am sure your father would say the same, were he here."

His friend's words silenced him immediately. His father had said exactly the same - and worse. Claveston sighed. "Please, behave yourself. I know what they said was not pleasant, but can you forgive it this once? For me? Do not spoil the fun."

William knew he had to suppress his displeasure. He was a guest and this was Wycliffe's party, not his own. He could not sway other's opinions with his ideals. He would have to endure them for now, but he vowed to always stand up for Mary, against their hurtful comments and behaviors.

As the time passed, it was all he could do to endure the conversation around him. He drank deeply of Wycliffe's claret, simply to keep himself from boredom. The women were insufferable. They thought only of themselves and their wealth. They clamored for the attentions of those men with titles greater than their own and ignored anyone they thought beneath them. It made William sick to his stomach, though he tried to be gracious. He smiled when expected and gave a nod when necessary, but spoke very little.

"Would you excuse me?" he asked the small group of people hovering around him when he could no longer take it. He waited long enough for acknowledgement before he strode away from them.

Claveston followed him. "Is everything all right?"

"Quite," William replied curtly.

"I know that tone," Claveston remarked. "You are not enjoying yourself. Come with me, I have yet to introduce you to Lady Margaret and her cousin, Miss Winslade? They are quite charming."

William looked into his friend's eyes and tried to muster a reassuring smile. "Enjoy the party, Wycliffe. I will be fine on my own."

"Are you sure?"

William nodded. "I am sure. I am thirty years old. I believe I can manage well enough."

Claveston chuckled. "I am but a year older and I still like an introduction."

Claveston was not an unlikeable man. But he was an entertainer, always ready to make the best of a situation - and to ensure that his guests had whatever they needed to enjoy themselves. He might not share their views, but he would never condemn them for having them.

"Go back to your guests. Everything will be well. I promise I will behave myself better, next time," William said with a tight smile.

"I will hold you to that," Claveston replied, and returned to his guests.

William crossed the room purposefully, his eyes fixed on the one person he wanted to speak to most, and whose side he should have gone to earlier. She was the only person here worth knowing.

Mary did not see him at first, but William could see no one else. How would she react to see him? Three years was a long time. How could he explain his absence? *I should have stayed in touch. I was a fool not to.*

"Miss Durand," he said with a smile as he bowed in greeting.

"My Lord." Mary curtseyed, lowering her eyes to the floor. William wished she would look at him. Her dark blue eyes were like sapphires, deep and dazzling.

He righted himself. "William, remember?"

Mary blushed, her cheeks turning an alluring pink. "Yes. William, I remember."

CHAPTER TWO

Even as she stood in the drawing-room of the Duke of Compton, watching the *crème de la crème* of Society present to enjoy this year's London Season, Mary felt no desire to mingle with any of them. To tell the truth, she found them snooty and unwelcoming at best. If she were to be brutally honest, she would much rather spend her time at home, in comfort, reading.

However, she had made a promise to her father - and she would help him in any way she could – even if that meant bearing the scorn of *The Ton*. Her father did not see what she had to endure at every event she had so far attended. It would break his heart to know how alone she felt and that there was nobody prepared to see past her lack of a title to see the woman she was.

Poor Papa. He had such hopes for their little family, and Mary hated that she might not be able to live up to those dreams he held, of her making a fine marriage. Because he had been welcomed, finally, by men of power and influence, he did not understand that it would take more than a townhouse in Mayfair, a fine gown and well-curled hair for Mary to be accepted. She was too old to be having her first Season, she was too gauche, had no powerful female friends or relatives to present her at court or petition the Lady Patronesses at Almack's for the necessary vouchers to attend – and she had committed the cardinal sin of coming from New Money.

She tried to lose herself in thoughts of the book she had been reading before she came out tonight, as she counted the minutes on the clock. The music was barely tolerable to her, even though the tune the string quartet was playing was a favorite of hers. Nothing seemed interesting about the evening, and it was all so loud that she could feel a headache coming on. She only wanted to leave but Mary knew that to do so would make her seem even more ill-mannered than those present already considered her to be.

Then she looked up, and amidst the faces that all seemed determined to mock her and make fun of her was one that caused her heart to melt. Her lips parted in silent surprise, that he was coming towards her. Mary had dreamed of William so often over the years since her time at Alnerton, that she felt she knew every tiny detail of his features by heart. Yet, the reality was far better than anything she had conjured up in her vivid imagination. His strong jaw and fine features, set off with a warm and delighted smile, captured her breath.

"You look well," William commented. "The years have been good to you."

Mary could hardly raise her eyes to answer him, but she tried her best to keep her voice even as she spoke. "Thank you, William. You look well, too."

He smiled. "I see that you have become ever more refined in my absence. You are quite the lady tonight. I could hardly believe it was you at first. It was my friend that confirmed your identity to me."

"Your friend?"

"The host of the party, Claveston St. John, the Earl of Wycliffe."

Mary nodded silently. She had been introduced to the young Earl upon her arrival at the house earlier that evening. Her father and the Duke of Compton had disappeared upstairs to discuss their interests with the duke's man of business, leaving her alone with Lord Wycliffe.

Their intention had been that Lord Wycliffe would introduce Mary to his acquaintances this evening, but the earl had obviously found himself more pleasantly occupied with others. A girl like Mary would not ever be important enough for his attention, it seemed. It seemed strange to her that such a man could be amongst William's friends.

The time she had spent at Caldor House would be etched in her heart and mind forever. Though she had been unwell, weak, and vulnerable, sharing the company of William and Charlotte had been such a blessing to her. She had been sure that she had found true friendship for the first time. Yet, though she had written often, letters from Alnerton had become more sparse, with barely a kindly wish at Christmas from Charlotte over a year ago, and nothing from William at all.

Mary had missed them terribly, but having her father back at last had, in some ways, made up for their loss. His return from America had been such a welcome change to her life – and it was thanks to William, who had found him and gotten him to come home, that she had been able to reunite with Papa on the docks at Tilbury.

"I have grown up in three years," she said with an awkward smile. "And learned so much. Father has allowed me to resume my studies under his guidance and instruction. I cannot tell you how grateful I am that Charlotte taught me so much about being a young lady while I was under your roof. Her lessons have served me well."

"I can see that. I think in many ways, you may have surpassed your teacher," William said gallantly.

"I doubt that," Mary said blushing. "How is dear Charlotte? I do hope she is well."

"Charlotte is well," William assured her. "Her wedding to James was a lovely event. She wished you could have been there."

"And I was sorry not to be able to attend. My father had just purchased our house, here in London, and he needed my presence to furnish it and make it a home," Mary explained.

"If you would permit me," William said politely, "I would write to her and tell her that I have seen you and pass on your regards?"

"I would be most glad of it. I have missed Charlotte very much, and regret that we have lost touch," Mary replied.

"I must confess my guilt, and beg your forgiveness," William said, hanging his head. "I did intend to write to you, Miss Durand. You must know that. However, things overwhelmed me and soon a week became a month, and then a year. Before I knew it three years passed without a word and I felt guilty to write after so long."

"There is nothing to forgive," Mary said generously. "I know just how busy your father keeps you."

He looked delighted at her pardon, and such a strong response startled her, but she could not consider the meaning. Her foolish feelings would only bring her harm. Was that not what Charlotte warned? William's future was not in his own hands. The Duke of Mormont would never accept her as good enough for William – and she knew it to be the truth. How could a girl such as her ever marry the son of a duke?

They stood together for a moment, a peculiarly comfortable silence that helped her to calm her nerves. "How is your father?" William asked her after some time had passed.

"He is well. Thank you for asking. He is here, upstairs, talking investments and the future with his Grace, the duke."

"Have you been enjoying yourself?" William asked, his eyes full of concern.

Mary wondered if he'd perhaps been party to some of the conversations that she had overheard here tonight - and felt ashamed that he might be somehow tarnished in the eyes of *The Ton*. She raised her gaze and smiled at the warmth in his whiskey-colored eyes. "Now I am," she admitted.

His smile was warm and tender, and a soft chuckle left his lips. "I am glad to hear it. I will admit that I was concerned when I saw you standing alone. I know how these affairs can be. Sometimes I feel like Society is made of different stuff to myself, and that I don't know how to behave amongst them."

"I can certainly agree to that," Mary admitted. It made her feel better to know William understood. "Charlotte gave me lessons on how to speak, and comportment – but being amongst these people, that is something I am having to learn as I go."

William nodded. "I have been amongst them my entire life, Miss Durand. I am still learning."

Mary's brow wrinkled. She could not imagine that

William ever suffered the discomforts she did. He was a respected part of a long-standing and esteemed family. He was perfectly suited to the company they now shared.

"I do not think so," Mary countered. "I cannot imagine you struggling to find your feet."

William stepped closer once more, inclining his head toward her. "Sometimes it is not your personage that makes you feel unwanted, but not sharing the beliefs of those around you. Sometimes, the ways of the company you keep can deeply disappoint you."

Mary studied his expression, wondering what he meant by that. What did others believe that he did not? He was brave to stand up for his beliefs over others. She was not sure she had the strength to do so. She had stood here, tonight, longing for just one person to approach her with an open mind and a kindly heart. And there had been only one. William.

"Never mind that," William said, obviously keen to talk about less difficult matters. "I would much rather hear about you and your father and would very much like to see him again. He was most interesting when we met at Tilbury, and I should love to converse with him once more. Do you think he would mind me joining them upstairs?"

She was glad to hear he wanted to meet her father again, but a part of her did not want him to go. She did not want to share William, he was the one glimmer of light she had for the evening, and she knew that if he left her it was very likely he would not return.

"Perhaps it would be better to wait until they are finished their business?" she suggested tactfully. "That way you can speak to Papa in private and have a more personal discussion, rather than getting caught up in all their talk of cans."

"You are right," William replied with a laugh. "I would only intrude. I am better off with my current company."

Heat erupted in her cheeks afresh at the compliment and the grin that accompanied it. Mary found herself unable to hold William's gaze. *Compose yourself, Mary. Do not make a spectacle of yourself in front of everyone here.* Eventually, she forced herself to look up. William was still looking down at her with kindly eyes. "Should you like a drink?" he asked her.

She nodded. "I believe there is a fruit punch available in the dining room."

"Give me one moment, I shall return immediately." He gave her a polite bow and disappeared into the crowd. Without him by her side, Mary felt awkward and uncomfortable again.

Unexpectedly a young woman, who looked only slightly older than herself, approached her, smiling warmly. She extended her hand. "Since we have no one to introduce us, we must do so ourselves. I am Fiona Whitchurch. And you are?"

Delight filled Mary's heart. Perhaps William's attentions had softened the opinions of at least some of those present. After all, he was an earl, and his father was a duke. His pedigree was impeccable, and if such a man considered Mary worth his time, perhaps others had come to that conclusion, too.

"I am Mary. Mary Durand. A pleasure to meet you." The pair bobbed curtsies to one another and Fiona stepped closer.

"The pleasure is mine. Are you a friend of Lord Wycliffe?"

"No," Mary answered truthfully. She knew it might be better to gild the truth a little, but it wasn't in her nature to do so. "His father, the duke, is one of my father's English investors."

"Truly? How fascinating," Miss Whitchurch said. "Perhaps my father knows him. He is involved in commerce."

Her chin raised infinitesimally as her smile brightened. If Miss Whitchurch's father was in commerce, then she was of the merchant classes, too. Perhaps there might be the hope of a friendship amongst these people after all.

"My father is Peter Durand, an inventor. He recently sold a patent for the creation of a new form of packaging."

"Packaging you said?" Miss Whitchurch said, looking surprised.

"Yes," Mary said, cautiously, noticing a change in the young woman's countenance. The fall of her smile and the shift of her gaze, from Mary to a small group of women standing not far away. Mary's joy at the possibility of making an ally diminished rapidly.

"Your father made his money through an invention? Is that correct?" Fiona asked again.

This time, Mary was not as eager to answer. She spoke cautiously. "Yes. The tin can."

Miss Whitchurch rolled her eyes and turned away from Mary, unable to stop herself from giggling. Mary's suspicions that all was not as it had initially seemed were proven correct. The young woman had not come to make her acquaintance, but to use her for the amusement of her friends, and Mary had fallen for the ruse. She lowered her eyes and bit back tears. She felt small and inadequate, unwanted, and despised.

Miss Whitchurch turned back to Mary her lovely face transformed by a malicious grin. "I did not believe what I had heard," she said, barely able to hide her derision.

"Please excuse me I need to return to my companions. We have more in common."

Mary could say nothing. She nodded and stepped back, wanting to be as far away as possible from the young woman and her giggling friends. But she would not give in to her misery. She had faced far worse than anything these silly girls could throw at her and survived. She held her chin high and vowed not to let their snobbery get to her.

Then she saw William returning to her side, and she suddenly didn't mind one bit that she might never be accepted amongst *The Ton*. As long as William was her friend, any torments could be borne – especially if he continued to look at her with such warmth and kindness.

However, it seemed that many of the guests had overheard her conversation with Miss Whitchurch. Of course, people were discrete, their glances fleeting and their whispered comments inaudible – but Mary could feel their judgment and their disdain. Mary tried to focus on William, but it was much harder to do, knowing that they were now being watched.

What if her connection to William would act as a detriment to his character? She could not live with herself to know that she was the cause of any trouble in his life, not after he had been so kind to her. Perhaps it would be better for him to leave her and rejoin his friends, but she could not bring herself to say the words.

William saw the look of concern on her face. "Do not regard them," he said supportively. "Society must have something to talk about, and anything will do. The gossips will always whisper – and their concerns will be forgotten in a week. Miss Whitchurch's father has made his money from shipping slaves and cotton – in my mind, your father's enterprises are far more honest and worthy of respect."

Mary knew he meant to ease her concerns, but she could not so easily discard them. She was not entirely surprised to learn that he was amongst those who did not deem the Trade to be in some way offensive. William was a kind man. But such an opinion was not as widely held as it perhaps should have been, Mary had learned, though it was perhaps not entirely surprising. Much of the wealth to be found in London came from those who had made their fortunes shipping slaves from Africa to the West Indies and bringing back cotton, sugar, and rum to England or had owned slaves themselves.

When she had learned of it, Mary had been aghast. To own another man, woman, or child seemed wrong to her – especially given her own childhood – but as was the case with so many other matters, her opinion did not seem to be much shared by those in Society. She was glad that William was of a mind with her. It confirmed to her his decency, not that she needed more than his treatment of her to know of that.

And, as it would seem, it mattered little that Miss Whitchurch was a merchant's daughter, that she too came from New Money - and that in Mary's mind, at least, that her fortune was tainted by the manner in which it had been accrued. Somehow, Miss Whitchurch had found a way to make a place for herself amongst these people and had become as hurtful to one like her as those born to privilege.

"Perhaps we ought not to give them something to talk about," she said sadly, looking up into William's kindly face. Mary did not want to be the subject of gossip, nor did she want anyone to speak ill of William because of his acquaintance with her. A man's reputation mattered greatly.

"Miss Durand, would you be more comfortable if I left you?" William asked, looking sad at the thought of it. "I would not want you to suffer any discomfort on my part."

She shook her head. "No, I am enjoying your company. I only want to spare you disparagement."

"Disparagement? Why would I suffer that? I am in as good a company as any. In many ways, better." William smiled at her sincerely.

Mary could not entertain negative thoughts when William looked at her. It was impossible. She sighed. Having him nearby would be lovely. Being under his protection would only make her life easier. Mary had thought it would be once she found her father, but their rise in society had proven more difficult than she could ever imagine. Acceptance seemed ever more remote than it had in her aunt and uncle's house.

She sipped her punch thoughtfully. William was being a true friend to her, yet again, and she would be loyal to him as long as he would allow it. Society might accept her one day, it might not - but until that day came, she now had someone to turn to.

"How long will you be in London?" she asked curiously, hoping he might say he'd be present for the entire Season. Without him, it would stretch out interminably.

"Only a few more days," he said, regret clear in his tone. "My father will not permit me absence from Alnerton for long. There is much to be done on the estate, and he must travel North soon to oversee our land holdings there."

Mary nodded, understanding all too well that the Duke of Mormont was not a man to be gainsayed. If he required

William's presence at Caldor House, then that was where William had to be, even if it saddened her greatly to know she would soon be alone again. "Your father needs you," she said sadly.

She barely heard the bitter laugh William gave, though he took such pains to hide it. "My father needs a lot, but I think my help is a far smaller necessity than you might think. Will you take a turn about the room with me?"

"Are you sure?" Mary asked, as a swarm of butterflies took off inside her belly.

"I am quite certain," William said with a smile. "Besides, it would be more conspicuous for us to be seen speaking alone so long than it would if we walked among the other guests. Perhaps I can introduce you to some of my acquaintances. Would you like that?"

Mary was not sure she wanted to meet his acquaintances after the way she had been treated by most of the guests here today, but she trusted William. He would not allow her to suffer embarrassment or disregard, she was sure of that. She smiled at him warmly. "I would like that very much."

CHAPTER THREE

After the party, William could not get Mary out of his mind. To see her there, in Wycliffe's drawing room, had been most unexpected, and he could not deny that she had changed very much for the better. He had written to his sister, Charlotte, in Edinburgh to tell her of it as soon as Wycliffe's party had come to a close. He was sure his sister would be pleased to hear that their former charge was doing well and was at least happy, now living with her father – even if she was not so content with the role of a young lady in Society. Charlotte would sympathize, she had never much cared for it, either.

Pity had driven him to take Mary home to Alnerton the first time he had seen her. She had been in such need and he simply couldn't walk on by and ignore that. Little had he known that such a decision would change his life forever. The moment he had seen that gaunt angelic face, so ashen and cold that she barely looked more than a corpse, he had known he had to help. It had been a feeling so strong that he could not deny it. But he had learned there was so much more to her.

William tried to make sense of his feelings for her. Why was her smile so much more radiant to him than anyone else's? Was it her innocence? Her kindness to everyone around her. Perhaps it was her inability to comprehend that others might wish to help her in return? Maybe it was simply that she was just perfect, in his eyes. Regardless of the reasons, all he wanted was to be near her. He longed to protect her from all hurts — and to keep her safe.

Though his remaining days in London were few, William was determined to see her again, and so he delivered a note to her home the very next morning, asking if he might call upon her. She replied that she would be delighted and, if he might consider it, that they could perhaps take a walk as the weather was so fine.

Warm breezes blew through Kensington Gardens as William waited for Mary's arrival. He was dressed comfortably for the weather in a dark green jacket, red floral-patterned silk vest, and plain cream breeches. He tipped his top hat to acquaintances as they went past on horseback, or on foot, enjoying the unusually sunny day.

William watched anxiously for her arrival. Every young woman descending from a carriage made his heart beat faster, only for her to lift her head and not be Mary. But when she finally did arrive, William wondered how he'd ever thought any one of those young women could have been Mary. She wore a neat straw hat, worn at a jaunty angle, her golden curls spilling out from under its brim, and an elegant grey walking dress with a matching maroon velvet spencer. But it was her smile, always her smile, that made his heart sing.

"William," she said, shyly ducking her head a little as she approached him.

He smiled at her and nodded politely to the young woman who walked slightly behind her. "Good day to you both, would you be so kind as to introduce us, Miss Durand?" he said looking at the young woman.

"Anne," Mary said happily. "This is my dear friend, Lord William Pierce, Earl of Cott. William, this is Anne Knorr, my lady's companion."

Miss Knorr dipped him a respectful curtsey. "It is an honor, my Lord," she said.

"The honor is mine," William said. "And please, my name is William."

Though a little saddened that things had changed and that he was not able to walk alone with Mary through the park, as they had once done at Caldor House, William was glad to see that Mary was accompanied. He had not even thought to ask if she might have a suitable chaperone and realized that such thoughtlessness on his part could only lead to more censure for Mary. He would need to do better.

His gaze lingered on Anne for a moment. She was a pretty little thing, with ruddy cheeks and dark hair peeking out from under a pretty blue bonnet. He wondered briefly how the two women had become acquainted, but this was not the time for such conversations.

"Shall we walk?" he asked, offering Mary his arm.

Mary nodded and tucked her delicate, gloved hand through the crook of his elbow. "Let's," she said eagerly.

It took no time at all for William to temper his stride to walk in time with Mary. Miss Knorr walked a few steps behind, offering them the semblance of privacy. "It is nice to see you out and about. London suits you," William said.

Mary looked up at him, a slight flush to her cheeks.

William wondered if it was from the fresh air and exercise, or his compliment. Whatever had cause it, it made her look radiant. "I am glad you think so, but I am not sure I agree. I feel very out of place here most of the time," she admitted.

"Where do you feel *in* place?"

Mary turned away, a gentle smile curving her lips as she considered his question. She didn't answer for a moment, giving William a chance to study her fine cheekbones and beautiful deep blue eyes. "Someplace far away from here," she said finally, "where good, kind people live - people who welcome me with open arms."

William couldn't help wondering if she was speaking about his home, and her time with them in Alnerton? Was that where she felt she belonged? William's heart could not help but find delight in the thought.

His eyes studied her closely. "I hope you can return to your special place someday."

Her eyes rose immediately, but hesitantly. "It would be a great gift," she said tentatively. "Though I do not see how it would be possible. Your father would never permit it."

"Your special place is Alnerton?" William confirmed, delighted that his home meant so much to her.

She nodded sadly. "I would so love to see Charlotte again - and meet her child. It would give me such pleasure."

William remained silent for a moment, a thought running through his head. With just himself and his father in residence at Caldor House, it would be most unseemly for a young woman to be seen to visit, alone — whether or not she had a lady's companion with her. There would need to be a woman to invite her and to host her stay. But there had to be a way he might make it happen?

He smiled, thinking that he would consult with Charlotte. She always knew what best to do. He would write to her as soon as he was alone. But now, he returned his fullest attention to the woman at his side. "I stand by what I said," he said softly, his voice a little hoarse with emotions he knew he shouldn't be feeling. "London suits you. You were made to walk in places like this, on days like this."

"You flatter me, William. That is not something you used to do," Mary commented, laughing lightly.

"Perhaps I should have," he admitted, though he knew he shouldn't be doing it now, either. No matter William's intentions, or his feelings for Mary, his father would never permit a match between them, and William had no intention of dishonoring Mary in any way. She deserved better than to be branded as a woman of easy virtue because of his actions.

Discomfort hovered between them. Desperate for safer ground, William changed the subject. "Charlotte's wedding was wonderful. Simple, just like she wanted. She and James have been very happy since." News of his sister's happiness seemed the easiest way to dispel the tension that had sprung up, unbidden between them. He glanced over his shoulder to where Anne walked behind them, her eyes downcast and her face expressionless. She hardly seemed present at all.

"I am glad to hear it," Mary replied, a soft sigh escaping her. "I wish I could have been there. I would have been so happy to celebrate their joy with them. How is little George?"

William chuckled, glad that the moment of discomfort

had well and truly passed. He could talk quite dotingly of his nephew's naughtiness for hours without pause. George was as rambunctious a youth as William had ever met. He was a glowing example of good health and happiness – and was the safest topic of conversation William could think of.

"He is very well. Growing fast." He laughed. "Enjoying his trip, I imagine. Charlotte and James have taken him with them to Scotland for a tour of the sights there, before she is too big to travel. They are expecting their first child."

Mary's eyes widened, full of delight. "A trip to Scotland? Another child?" William nodded. "How wonderful. Charlotte truly is blessed. I would love to be so fortunate," she added wistfully.

William was certain that Mary had not travelled much. In truth, her flight to Alnerton, in the hopes of finding her father, and the subsequent trip to Tilbury to meet her father at the docks had probably been the extent of her experience outside of Leicestershire, where she had grown up. He found himself thinking he would like to take her to Scotland, and to Europe, to show her the sights that had been such marvels to him. He imagined them walking in the rugged Highlands, and through the streets of Paris - then the image changed. As unexpected as it was perfect, William's mind had conjured an image of Mary, swollen with child, smiling brightly as she walked the lawns of Caldor House. He blinked the vision away, knowing such a thought could never come to pass.

He looked ahead and spoke quickly, trying to rid his mind of the image that had seemed all too real. "My sister is enjoying her life," he gushed, "much more than I ever believed possible. James is a good man though he was a fool for too long. While they live in contentment and happiness, I find that doing my father's bidding keeps me too busy to think of much else." A wry smile curved his lips. To one who didn't know, it might appear that Charlotte's life was easy and blessed. Little did they know how hard she'd fought to win and keep the man she loved.

But even if he fought for Mary, William knew he would never be allowed to win her. Father would not permit such a match. William would marry in a way that would benefit the duchy – not himself and his happiness. A match would be decided upon that would serve his father's purposes, to increase their landholdings and their wealth – and William would have no say in the matter.

"Even now?" Mary questioned. "Here, in the park, you are considering all you must do for the estate?"

"Not now," William answered, smiling. "Today, I have promised myself that I shall live in the moment."

Mary smiled. "I am glad."

"William, do you think that *The Ton* will ever accept someone like me? Someone not born to wealth and property?"

William wanted to tell her yes that society would eventually accept her, but that would be a lie. There were those who would never accept Mary nor anyone of her family, no matter how much money they had or the connections she might make. She would always be unwelcomed, left on the outskirts, abandoned by 'good society'. Yet there were those who had crossed the divide. Young women like Miss Whitchurch, whose vast fortunes and extensive holdings in the West Indies made them a fine catch for impoverished earls, viscounts, and even dukes. It was hard to predict who might be accepted, and who might not.

"I can tell your answer, even without you speaking," Mary muttered. He wasn't sure if she was sad or angry.

"Miss Durand, it isn't what you think," he said wishing there was more he could do to ease her passage into Society himself.

"I have tried for three years to fit into Society," Mary said, looking up at him, anger blazing in her eyes. "I have learned their ways. Father saw to that. I speak like them. I dress like them. I dine in the same places as they do and have better table manners than most of them. Yet, still, they look at me as if I was nothing, and my father even less than that because of what he does."

This time his hand could not resist the urge to reach out and touch. William placed his hand gently upon her forearm, hoping the small gesture would give some comfort. "They are fools."

"Are they? Or am I the fool to think that I might ever belong here?" Mary said bitterly. "You do not know how lonely it can be here, William. Even with Anne beside me, I feel as if I am on another planet without the understanding of another soul."

"You are not alone, Miss Durand. You do have friends here and especially in Alnerton." He smiled at her warmly.

"I miss Alnerton. I think I was happy there. Sometimes, I even miss Leicestershire - though not the home of my aunt and uncle, but the people I knew there when my mother was alive before Papa went away. The society was low, but they were far friendlier and more welcoming to others than those I have found here."

"We all missed you once you were gone," William admitted, hoping it might cheer her mood. She seemed so lost, so sad – and rightfully angry at the way she had been treated. "Those months you spent with us changed the entire household, for the better I might add, and you were missed once you were gone. Charlotte, especially, missed your company."

"I expect James helped remedy that," Mary said, a weak smile forming as she tried to let go her hurts.

William chuckled. "Yes, my dear friend always has had a knack for distracting her, but it does not take away from the fact that you were missed."

"Thank you, William. That helps. I know your father did not so easily bear my presence. He would agree with many of those I have met here in London, no doubt, that I am seeking a position above my station in life and should be content with my lot."

"Father bears the presence of few, including his own children," William mused.

"That I very much doubt," Mary said kindly. "After all, you are his son and the heir to everything he has. It makes for a very appealing presence. Certainly more than someone who is taking his hospitality with no means of repaying it."

"I believe you have repaid the service we paid you far more than you imagine," he corrected her. "Far more."

Mary looked at him curiously, her brow furrowing delicately. "Whatever do you mean? I did nothing. I have thought of what I could do, but nothing seemed sufficient. I know my father feels the same. We would do anything to repay your kindness – especially the time and expense you must have gone to reunite us when Papa returned from America."

"It is what a good friend does," he said softly. "And your friendship is, to me, worth more than any gift or repayment that you could ever offer. Charlotte would say the same, I am sure of it."

Mary blushed. "You have so many friends. I doubt that my friendship makes much difference."

How little she knew or could possibly imagine. William knew many people, but few had made such an impression upon his heart and mind as Mary had – both before at Alnerton, and here, now. Hers was s truly special soul, unselfish, kind, and sensitive. She was too good for this world, and that was what those of *The Ton* would always sense and be afraid of. It was why they would never fully accept her – as they would never understand how someone who had experienced such terrible things could still be kind and decent and worry more for others than she did herself. They saw their own venality reflected back by her goodness and couldn't bear it.

"Do not be troubled by those you meet" he said to her firmly. "They may not all see your worth, but others will. Focus on those that can see past the external trappings. Those are the ones who matter most. In Society, you cannot always tell friend from foe, it is why I rarely travel to London for the Season. It is a nest of vipers waiting to strike. It is better to stay close to those you can be sure of."

"How will I know those I can trust from those I cannot?" Mary questioned.

"I will help you. I will introduce you to people I class amongst my friends whilst I am here. Trust me, I would not put you in the company of anyone I would not trust to take care of you, as if you were my own sister," William assured her.

Mary smiled brightly. "I wish you were staying longer. I could use more talks like this when I feel down."

William hooked his arm and Mary slipped hers into it. "Then we will make the most of the time we have."

They continued through the park, the warm breeze carrying the delicate floral aromas with it. It was relaxing for him to walk beside her. William turned, Mary was looking at the roses they passed, her gaze distracted by the flowers. He was glad for it. It allowed him to watch her unnoticed.

If only they could stay like this forever, just the two of them, walking and talking together. He liked their talks. Mary was innocent, maybe even naïve, but she was honest and true. He liked that. He wanted that in his life. It was so refreshing. Yet, he lived under the constant reminder of expectation, and the cruel injustice of obligation – and knew that his friendship with Mary could be easily trampled upon by those obligations.

He would do what he could for Mary while he had the chance. Soon, he would be forced to return to Alnerton and, as always, he would do what was expected of him. Who knew when they would see each other again? Would it be another three years? Longer? Would she find love and marry during that time? Despite knowing how hard it would be for him to see her with another man, William hoped so. She deserved every happiness and more.

CHAPTER FOUR

The Durand household, at number four Halkin Street, may have been small compared to the grand townhouses on fashionable Belgrave Square just yards from their door, but Mary was sure their home held more life and warmth than any of them. After everything she had been through, the elegant townhouse was a palace, and she had done all she could to make it not just a home for Papa and herself, but for their household staff as well. She remembered all too well the misery of life below stairs and had been determined to make sure their small staff always knew how valued and important they were.

Since moving into one of London's more fashionable districts, life had been infinitely better than she could ever have imagined, whilst she was still trapped in the home of her aunt, but it had remained lonely and cut off in many ways. Since William's return to her life, everything seemed better. Each day held greater surprises, and she was beginning to believe that she could be happy in London – though she was acutely aware of his imminent departure and couldn't help feeling concern that once he was no longer there, that things would return to the way they had been before.

It seemed that William had been right. Knowing the right people was the key to happiness in the bustling city. Though he was only in town for a short time, William went out of his way to introduce Mary to his friends, and amongst them, she had found acceptance, at least for now. She would be eternally grateful for William's kindness in making the introductions because she now had some hope that even when he was gone that she would have acquaintances to spend time with who cared little for her life before, and who thought her father's pursuits were admirable.

"Well good morning," Papa said as Mary kissed her father's head in a morning greeting as she and Anne joined him at the breakfast table.

"And good morning to you," Mary replied as she helped herself to the buffet set out on the sideboard and took her seat to his right. Anne soon followed, taking the seat on the left. Papa looked at them both proudly from his place at the head of the table.

"You look different," Papa said, looking at Mary more closely. "You have been elated these days past, happier than I have ever seen you – but today, not so much."

Mary sighed. William was to leave for Alnerton today, and she could hardly bear the thought of being here without him. He had made everything so much better for her, but his presence gave her confidence and brought her happiness that she had never dared to dream might be possible. "I am a little sad, is all," she said, trying to make light of it.

Papa gave her a gentle smile, taking her hand and

patting her knuckles tenderly. "I have been so glad to see you so content, and it concerns me that you should be so sad, though I think I can guess why."

She could feel her cheeks warm at her father's observations, the image of William immediately coming to mind. She tried to force a smile, but it was useless. The thought of William leaving always elicited the same reaction from her. The ideas she had let roam in her mind in recent days, of her and William together were an indulgence she knew she should not entertain, but she could not help herself. He was so kind and generous – and had done all in his power to improve Mary's standing in Society. He had saved her life – again. She could hardly bear the thought he might not be there to care for her and shepherd her through the tribulations of the rest of the Season.

Mrs Derby, the housekeeper stepped inside the room holding a small silver salver. She coughed politely to announce her presence. "Sir, there is a gentleman come calling." A plump woman, with kindly eyes and fastidious attention to detail, she had proven time and again to be the perfect choice to head their small household staff. She stepped forward and proffered the tray.

Papa picked up the ivory calling card, embossed with gold lettering and smiled. Mary raised her eyebrows quizzically. "Who is it, Papa?" she asked.

"As if you do not recognize this card out of a hundred like it," Papa teased.

"William?" Mary queried, as her heart leaped in her chest, her stomach knotting immediately at the mere thought of his presence – especially as she had not expected to see him this day.

Papa smiled at Mary, then turned to his housekeeper. "Please, show Lord Cott into the drawing room," he instructed Mrs Derby who nodded and bobbed a small curtsey.

Papa offered Mary his arm and the two of them made their way from the breakfast room across the grand hall-way, with its marble-tiled floor and imposing oak staircase, and entered the drawing-room. Anne followed them, without saying a word. Someone had lit the fire, and the elegant room was warm and inviting, with bright sunlight pouring in through the high windows. Mary took a seat on one of the sofas by the fire, as Papa reached for his pipe on the mantle and began to fill it with tobacco. Anne took one of the window seats, where she pulled out a book and began to read.

William strode confidently into the room. As ever, Mary felt her breath catch in her lungs. How could a man be so breathtaking? Yet, William was. She tried to still her rapidly beating heart by taking a couple of slow breaths and rose to greet him.

Papa stepped forward to greet the younger man. "My Lord," he said politely. The two men gave one another a polite bow.

"William, please," William corrected. "We are friends of old, are we not?"

Her father laughed and Mary knew he was recalling the first time these two men had met, on the busy docks at Tilbury upon Papa's return from America. They had fallen into easy conversation over supper at the inn that night, no concern between them as to the disparity of their circumstance. "Aye, yes. William," Papa said warmly as the two men shook hands like old friends. "I will try to remember that, but I am afraid I am accustomed to the formalities of London now."

"There should be no formalities between us," William

assured him, as he glanced past Papa and smiled at Mary, offering her a bow. "And how lovely you look today, Miss Durand."

Mary bobbed him a curtsey and smiled back, trying to suppress a giggle. She found it more than amusing that William always insisted that they not use his title, or call him my Lord – yet he insisted upon honoring them with theirs. "Thank you, William," she said. "What a pleasant surprise. I thought you were due to return to Alnerton this morning."

"I leave this afternoon," William said. "I hope you do not mind the unannounced visit. I was in the area and wanted to stop in and pay my respects before my departure."

Her father indicated that William should take the armchair by the fire, as he took a seat beside Mary on the couch. "That is kind of you, my Lord – William," Papa corrected himself with a grin.

William chuckled. "It is quite all right. I know I am unusual in wishing to leave aside such formalities."

"You are most certainly unlike many of your class," Papa agreed wholeheartedly.

William looked delighted at the comment. Mary loved to see him so content. But it seemed that she was alone in wanting to know why William had called, and so early. It was quite unheard of to attend a lady at breakfast. One's card might be left, and an arrangement to call made for later in the day, so this was most unusual. Unconsciously, she tapped her foot and frowned a little.

William noticed and smiled. "Mr Durand, I am sorry to call at such an early hour, but I wished to meet with you before I depart, as we have not been able to do so whilst I was in town. Miss Durand tells me that you have made quite the adjustment to life in London, and your business is doing well – and I can see that you are quite settled here, in this lovely home."

Mary was touched at William's kindness. She could see the pride swell in her father's breast as he raised his chin to answer. "Exceedingly. Mary has made it quite the place," he said patting her hand. "And I think you know that I am in discussions with the Duke of Compton and his man of business, to bring the patent that brought me such success in America, into the English market."

"Excellent," William exclaimed. "I congratulate you. I am sure all will go well. The Duke of Compton is a shrewd man, and his man of business even more so. He will not steer you wrong."

Papa beamed, obviously glad of such a character reference for his prospective partners. "Thank you. It gives me more confidence in the arrangement to hear you say that."

"I speak as I see it and know that the Duke is an honest man – and a very successful one, too. I have known him most of my life – and my father and much of *The Ton* often follow where Compton leads," William replied.

"Would you like some tea, Father? William? I can have Mrs. Derby bring some," Mary suggested as the two men continued to discuss matters of business.

"No thank you, Mary," her father replied. "Though I do favor some of that marvelous lemonade you made."

"That sounds delightful," William added. "Lemonade is so refreshing on a warm day."

"Then it is settled," Papa said happily. "Anne, would you fetch it through?"

Anne stood up, nodding, but Mary indicated she should sit back down. "It is no trouble, I can go," she said and got up to leave the room. William and Papa both rose from their seats until she had left, which made her smile. To be treated like a lady was still new to her, and occasionally made her feel quite uncomfortable – but such touches were a delight.

She decided to go down to the kitchen herself, rather than calling for Mrs Derby or the parlor maid. Cook was busy kneading dough, her face red with exertion, and flour dusting her grey hair. "Carry on," Mary said to her as Cook made to take off her apron and move towards her. "I can fetch a tray myself."

Cook gave her a grateful nod and went back to her bread-making. Mary pulled out a silver tray, upon which she set a jug of lemonade, four glasses, some fruit tarts, a sponge cake, and the plates and forks to eat them from. She made her way cautiously back upstairs and into the drawing room where she set the tray upon the table between the two men and began to pour out the lemonade.

William drank deeply, then beamed at Mary "This is delicious. Not too sweet and not too tangy. Just right." Mary smiled shyly, filled with pride that he had so enjoyed it.

"Would you like a tart, or a slice of cake?" she said, glad of the formalities, so she could keep her countenance.

"I should like a piece of that cake," William admitted, "though it is barely past breakfast."

"I should, too," Papa agreed.

Mary cut them both a slice, arranging them carefully upon the plates, before handing them to her father and to William. She gave each of them a fork, then turned to where Anne was still reading quietly. "Should you like a piece? Or I have brought up the fruit tarts I know you love," she asked her companion.

Anne looked up from her book. "I should love a tart," she admitted. "And a glass of lemonade, if I may." She moved to fetch them, then retreated to her nook.

Mary sat back on the sofa and watched as Papa and William talked enthusiastically about all manner of matters. She barely understood a word of much of it, but it didn't stop her from taking pleasure in William's soft baritone and the delight evident on Papa's face to be talking with the younger man. Her father was enjoying himself in a way she had not seen in some time. She did not want it to end.

Time passed too swiftly. The clock struck midday. William glanced up at the clock. "I should be on my way," he said getting to his feet.

"We have kept you," Papa said, chagrined.

"Not at all. I have enjoyed a most pleasant morning," William said. "It is only that I must eat before I take my leave for the country."

"I do not know if it would be proper, William, but should you care to join us for luncheon?" Papa asked immediately. "We can continue our conversation, and you can leave immediately after."

William glanced in Mary's direction as if seeking permission, though she had noted that his eyes had lit up at the idea of staying a few hours longer. Mary nodded, smiling. She could think of nothing she would like more than a further two hours of William's company.

William took her meaning and turned back to Papa. "I would be honored."

"Then I shall inform Cook immediately and get Mrs Derby to set another place," Papa said, and disappeared.

With Papa's departure, the atmosphere in the room changed. No young woman could ever be left alone in the company of a man, but Mary had almost forgotten that Anne was still in the room, she'd been so quiet. The tension was almost unbearable as she waited to see what William might say or do. His eyes were fixed upon her face, and it made her duck her head to avoid the intensity of his gaze.

As the moments ticked by, with neither of them speaking, Mary raised her eyes to William's, wondering how many acts of kindness would need to be repaid. His kindness in taking time to spend with Papa, even though he had so little of it was just one of the things that showed his impeccable character. His generosity to her, his warmth, and his determination to help her to fit into the Society she now found herself a part of – as well as owing him her life – it was all too much.

The tolling of a bell called them to luncheon. "May I walk you to the dining room?" William asked, as he got to his feet and offered her his arm.

Mary smiled, stood up, and took his arm. They walked across the hallway into the dining room, Anne walking behind as always. The table was elegant but simple. Mrs. Derby had laid out their best china and crystal, in honor of their guest. Papa had given up his place at the head of the table, in honor of William's higher rank, and had taken the seat at the foot. Mary and Anne sat on either side, between the two men. Thankfully, the table was not too large, and the men were able to continue their lively conversation without needing to raise their voices.

Mary barely noticed how even a morsel of the food served to her tasted. She was too focused upon William's enjoyment of the meal. He ate with relish, and as he laid down his napkin at the end of the meal, he beamed and patted his stomach. "Give my compliments to the cook," he said. "This was the finest meal I have had in London."

"Surely not," Mary replied. "You have sat at far finer tables than this."

William turned to her, his expression calm and pleasant. "I was not speaking of the meal alone, but of the company. Sometimes those present make the food all the more edible."

"Not to mention it aids in digestion," her father mused. "Mary, the lemon pie was delicious, my dear. You are to be congratulated."

"You made the dessert?" William asked, looking at Mary with admiration.

"Papa," Mary interjected as a blush heated her cheeks. "You praise me too highly."

"Not anywhere near enough, I fear," her father countered, a tear in his eye and his voice choked with emotion. "I have so many years of praise to make up for. I do not think I will ever be able to make up for the time lost. You are far more accomplished than I ever imagined you could be."

"Papa, I am your daughter. I am what you have helped me become."

"No. I cannot claim to be responsible for all that you have made of yourself," Papa insisted. "You are to be credited with it all."

"I think there is another, who also played a part," Mary said modestly, as her cheeks flushed red with embarrassment. "Dear Charlotte, William's sister, began my education, and it is her example I have tried to follow. She was a true friend to me in my time at Alnerton, as was dear William."

William smiled, a faint blush coloring his cheeks, too.

"Thank you, Miss Durand. I believe Charlotte would be delighted to know she has played such an important role in your life," he said, as he adroitly passed over the compliment she had paid to him.

"Though this has been a most pleasant way to spend a morning, I really must take my leave of you," William said sadly. "However, Mr Durand, I should very much like to invite you both, and dear Miss Knorr, of course," he nodded towards Anne who flushed bright red under his gaze, "to visit with my family in Alnerton, at your earliest convenience. Charlotte returns from her Scottish tour in just a few weeks - and I know she would love to see Miss Durand again and would be delighted to make your acquaintance, Sir."

Mary could barely contain her delight. She turned to her father, eyes wide and holding her breath as she waited for his answer. She could barely believe that she was to be offered the opportunity to visit Alnerton again. It was too good to be true. Papa met her gaze, and smiled indulgently, but shook his head sadly.

"I cannot tell you how honored I am by such an invitation, William," Papa explained. "But I am afraid that will not be possible at this time. I must return to America to deal with some matters of outstanding business there. I leave in just over a week's time."

Mary's hopes were dashed to smithereens. She would not be going to visit her friends, and nor would she be blessed to see the place that had nurtured her body and spirit back to health. Anne gave her an understanding smile as Mary met her eye.

Her father was not yet finished. "However," he added. "I do not see why Mary and Anne could not join you, once your sister returns to Caldor House, of course. Mary has spoken so often of Charlotte and her son, George, that I am sure she would like to see them again."

Mary's felt her soul fill with delight. "Do you mean it, Father?"

"Of course, my dear. I know I spend much of my time thinking about my inventions and my business, I am not unaware of the esteem you hold for the people kind enough to take care of you when your need was greatest. We can never possibly repay them for their generosity, though I hope someday to find a way to do so."

"There is no need, sir," William said respectfully. "Miss Durand was a delight, and we would gladly do the same again – were it necessary."

"I am aware of that," Papa said. "But it does not take away the obligation I owe."

"Sending Miss Durand back to us would go a long way to paying that debt," William assured him.

"And would please my Mary, I don't doubt," Papa turned to Mary and smiled. "Though you have had William in your company these past days, I am sure you would like to see Charlotte, too." He stood up and took William's hand, shaking it firmly. "And in truth, it will leave me beholden to you, my Lord, once more. I would not be happy leaving Mary here alone and the voyage to America is not fit for a young lady, at least not on a cargo ship. I think Alnerton would be a better option for her."

"Then it is settled," William commented. "You will travel to America, and my family will look after Miss Durand and Miss Knorr at Alnerton. How long will you be away for?"

"Three or four months, perhaps, depending upon the speed of the passage," Papa said thoughtfully. "Though I could not ask you to watch over Mary for that long," her father countered.

"Nonsense. It would be our pleasure to have her with us, and to see her safely home again when you return." William looked utterly delighted at the news and Mary felt a flush of happiness at seeing him so content. It seemed unreal, but it was. She was going back to Alnerton. She would once again walk the gardens and be amongst those she cared for the most in the world, other than her Papa.

"Miss Anne, have you ever been to Alnerton?" her father asked.

"No, sir. Never," Anne said softly. She looked pleased to be included in the discussion, though.

"Then you are in for a treat," Papa said happily. "Mary tells me nothing but good things about the place. I am sure she will take great pains to show you around. Is that not so?" Her father grinned at them both and drank the last of his wine.

Mary nodded, but she was looking at William. She remembered every detail of the time she had spent in his home. Each rosebush and lane he had shown her, each book he had read to them all each evening after supper. Each smile and kind word. She would share with Anne the beautiful places that lay all around Caldor House - but she could not guarantee that Anne could ever experience the other pleasures that Mary had enjoyed in her time there.

CHAPTER FIVE

A *lnerton, Bedfordshire, 1818*

THE WEEKS BETWEEN LEAVING LONDON AND THE arrival of Mary and Anne at Caldor House passed too slowly. William personally oversaw every tiny detail, ensuring that the house and gardens were at their very best - driving his household staff to distraction and making Charlotte laugh out loud when she and James returned from their tour of Scotland to find him fretting about which tablecloth to use on what would be the young women's first night at Alnerton.

Thankfully, Father was still preoccupied with matters on their lands in the North and was unsure of when he would be returning, which would only make things easier for them – and for him. If he had not been in the North, there was no earthly circumstance in which he would have dared to invite Mary to Alnerton. There was no doubt in

William's mind that his father would disapprove but William was willing to accept the consequences he might have to pay later so that he could spend some time with Mary now.

In his dreams, he harbored the hope that perhaps if his father saw her as she was now, that he would change his mind – that he might see that Mary would make a suitable addition not just to the society that the family kept, but to the family itself. It was unlikely, but William had to hold onto the hope that one day he might be free to make such a choice for himself – and have his father approve.

William caught the attention of the housekeeper as she passed him in the corridor. "Mrs. Churchill, is everything ready?"

The older woman looked at him with a placid expression. "I have already prepared everything as you asked. The first time, the second, and now the third." Her tone was a little brusque, but she smiled at him kindly. "Everything is perfect for the ladies' arrival, though Lady Charlotte sent a message that she was a little delayed, as George has been grizzling all morning."

William knew he was fussing too much – and was causing his staff to feel anxious because of it. "I am sorry, Mrs. Churchill," he said, chastened. "You know perfectly well how to do your job without my assistance. I apologize if I seemed to doubt you."

"My Lord, you are entitled to do as you wish," Mrs Churchill said. "There is no need to apologize." The older woman bowed her head politely. "If that will be all, I need to go to the kitchens, to ensure that luncheon is on schedule."

William nodded. "Yes, of course."

He paced up and down the hallway, as he awaited the

arrival of Mary's carriage. His palms were slightly sweaty and his breathing quickened. She was due to arrive at any moment. The month that passed from their last meeting and today felt far too long. William peered out the window, just in time to see a carriage coming up the drive.

The thundering in his chest was immediate. William walked to the door, pulling it open before the butler or Mrs. Churchill could do so. He stepped out on the stone terrace, the sun shining brightly on him as he descended the steps to meet the smart black carriage.

He admired the perfectly matched pair as they approached, their long strides shortening as they came to a halt just in front of him. The coachman stepped down, but William was first to the carriage door, a smile bright on his face as he pulled it open and held out his hand to assist them in climbing down. "Miss Durand. Miss Knorr. Welcome to Caldor. My sister will join us shortly; she sent word that she is running a little late."

Mary took his hand and stepped out of the carriage, her foot clad in delicate pale blue slippers that matched her dress. Lustrous curls framed her angelic face, a small smile parting her lips as she looked up at him with clear, bright eyes and curtseyed. "My lord." He frowned, but then he noticed the teasing look she gave him along with her formal greeting. He grinned back.

Miss Knorr followed Mary, and William offered them both an arm. They tucked their hands through the crooks of his elbows, and he led them up the ornamental stone steps, through the ornate double doors and across the vast hallway into the sunny front parlor.

Mrs. Churchill had laid out some light refreshments for afternoon tea upon the dresser, and he offered them both some lemonade. "It is perhaps not quite so good as your own, but refreshing nonetheless," he said as Mary moved forward to pour for them all, her cheeks flushed at his intended compliment.

William smiled as Mary prepared a plate of cucumber sandwiches, and other tidbits for him and Anne, then one for herself. She was an excellent hostess and had fallen into her customary role as easily as she smiled.

"How was the journey?" he asked as they all took a seat by the fire.

"A lot longer than I remembered," Mary replied with a smile, "and considerably more bumpy." Everyone laughed. "However, the beautiful countryside made up for it. I knew the moment we entered the county. Did I not say so, Anne?"

The young woman nodded quickly as she tried to swallow the bite of her sandwich that she'd barely taken as Mary spoke. "Yes. Yes, you did."

"I am happy you remembered it so well after so long," William replied. "I was not sure that you would."

"I remember everything about this place."

The sincerity in Mary's eyes made him smile. It had a strange effect on him knowing that her time there meant so much to her that she remembered it all so clearly. "I look forward to showing you much more of the area," he said to them both. "When Miss Durand was here before she was most unwell," he explained to Anne. "I hope to be able to show you all the places we were unable to see before."

"I look forward to it. We both do," Mary said eagerly.

"Yes, of course," Anne agreed. "I have been looking forward to this trip. Miss Durand has told me many good things of this place and the people here."

"I hope we shall be able to live up to them," William said softly.

Mary tucked a stray strand of her hair behind her ear. William was mesmerized by it, such a tiny action, yet so elegantly done.

"I am sure you will," she said shyly. "I have every confidence in you to show Anne the same hospitality that you showed me."

William forced his eyes away from the delicate features he found so beguiling, and instead focused upon Anne Knorr. Showing partiality was not something he wanted to do; after all, they were both guests in his home and were therefore due the same attention and consideration. And, as a lady's companion, Anne was probably often overlooked. He knew that she and Mary had grown close. It would please Mary if he were to include Anne more, he was sure of it.

"Miss Knorr, I must apologize to you," he said earnestly. "I did not get to know you that well, whilst we were all in London. It would please me greatly if we might remedy that, now?"

Anne nodded politely. "That would be most pleasant," she said nervously, as she took another bite of her sandwich.

"Might I ask what part of the country you hail from?" William asked.

Anne fumbled with her napkin, almost dropping it, as she attempted to wipe her lips clean of crumbs. "My family is from a small town in Exeter called Tulilly. My father is baronet. Keating Knorr, my lord. Have you heard of him?"

William tried to recall if he had ever heard the name before, but there were so many baronets, earls, and dukes in England that it was difficult to keep track of them all. "I am sorry, I have not."

Anne smiled, but William could see the disappointment in her eyes. He did not want her to feel uncomfortable, so he did the only thing he could.

"However, should I ever be in that part of the country I would be pleased to make his acquaintance," William answered. "Perhaps you will introduce me?"

The smile on Anne's face proved he had been right to offer her his attention, and to offer the connection. "It would be my pleasure to, my Lord. My father is a great admirer of the duke, your father."

William was delighted to have so easily pleased the young woman, and he would do all in his power to ensure that her family had a better acquaintance with his family, even though getting his father to agree to any such thing might prove impossible. "I will see to it that the two of them might meet."

Afternoon tea complete, William could see that the women were both tired. "I believe your rooms should be ready for you," he told them as he set his plate down on the table. "I know the trip was a long one and, I think I have occupied you enough for the moment." He stood up and rang a bell by the mantel. Mrs Churchill appeared in the doorway and bobbed a curtsey to the two young women. "Mrs Churchill will see you to your rooms."

Mary and Anne stood and made to follow Mrs Churchill, who led them out into the hallway. William tarried a little behind them. Mrs Churchill mounted the stairs, and Mary was about to follow when a loud cry came from just outside. "Oh, dear Mary, you've arrived − and before we could be here ourselves." Charlotte burst into the hallway and ran to Mary, who looked delighted as his sister wrapped her arms around her lost friend.

The two women smiled and laughed as tears poured down their cheeks. It pleased William to see them reunited. He knew that Charlotte had been very fond of Mary and had missed her terribly once she had departed to join her father. James appeared behind his wife, holding George's hand. He looked a little awkward, even though he had been introduced to Mary when she had been at Caldor before.

James had been a soldier and had suffered severe scarring in battle. He was sensitive about his appearance, but William knew that Mary would soon put him at ease. She was not the type to judge anyone by their appearance, but by the contents of their hearts – and William was sure that Anne was much the same. His brother-in-law had little to fear from their sweet-natured guests.

George ran towards his Uncle and William swept him up off his feet, high above his head and twirled the boy around. Everyone laughed as the boy squealed his delight. "I have missed you, little man," William said fondly as he brought the lad down and hugged him tightly.

"And he has missed you," Charlotte said. "So, if you don't mind, I shall leave the three of you," she looked from her husband to her brother, to her son, "so I might get Mary and her friend settled in, and so we may catch up on all of each other's news."

William grinned as Charlotte shepherded her charges up the stairs, dismissing Mrs Churchill. She was a real force of nature, and woe betide anyone that stood in her way – even Father.

William had not ever been so bold. He'd grown up with his responsibilities at the forefront of his mind. Everything he did had been laid out and planned for him, before he was even born. Because of that, he had always told himself that falling in love was useless. Charlotte had been fortunate to find such a thing – and been permitted to keep hold of it - but she was not their father's son. She was his daughter, and that was a very different circumstance.

William wanted to be different. He longed to be as bold as Charlotte had been when she'd insisted upon her marriage to James – despite Father's intentions otherwise. Sometimes, he wished he had been born without a title, into some other family so that he could be free to live as he wished. It was a silly fantasy and one he had not considered for some time – at least he hadn't dwelled on it much until seeing Mary again.

Mary had changed everything. She was perfect in his eyes and he would look on her forever if he could. But there could be no future for them, as Father would never permit a match – no matter how good Mary's fortune might be. Father did not need him to marry a merchant's daughter to shore up the family inheritance. The Mormont fortune was quite sufficient. Father was proud and old-fashioned. He would accept nothing less than the daughter of a duke for his son. Rank mattered to Father.

William turned his attentions to his brother-in-law and nephew. "Shall we go to the stables?" he asked. "I think that the horses have missed you whilst you went on your adventures. Should you like a riding lesson, whilst you tell me all about your time in Scotland?"

The little boy's eyes were wide. "Yes, please," he said excitedly.

"You spoil him," James warned William.

"I know, but as his uncle and not his father, surely that is my place?" William said with a grin.

"I suppose that may be true enough," James agreed. "To the stables it is."

The rest of the afternoon passed swiftly enough, but for William, it felt like an eternity to wait until he might see Mary at dinner. Having George there, to distract him – and to remind him how much he longed for a child of his own – was a blessing. He was glad that Charlotte and James had been so amenable to joining him at Caldor House for the duration of Mary's visit.

He had been determined that the proprieties were upheld. The last thing he wished to do was to add to Mary's troubles by impugning her honor in any way. A lengthy stay in the home of two unwed men might easily have set tongues wagging. He had seen at first hand just how cruel the jibes and taunts directed Mary's way had been. She had received censure she did not deserve. He would do nothing to give grist to the gossip mill. Mary's visit to Alnerton could not be in any way improper. Asking his sister to be present meant he would have to share Mary – but it would at least ensure that tongues didn't wag in London.

CHAPTER SIX

The sun was warm on her skin, but it wasn't the exertion of the unexpectedly competitive bowls match that was making Mary's heart beat so quickly. It was William's presence and his constant attention. In the two weeks since their arrival at Caldor House, Mary had experienced nothing but joy. Time spent with Charlotte and dear little George was a pleasure, even the quiet and often taciturn James was becoming less so. But it was moments like this one, where she was able to spend time, almost alone, with William that brought her the most pleasure.

She had been unutterably relieved when she arrived to find the duke absent. She had so worried about his reaction to her presence, but William continued to assure her that she had nothing to fear. Mary still harbored her doubts, but she was prepared to enjoy her time at Caldor for as long as it might last.

"I shall win this one," Mary declared as she picked up her first ball and prepared to launch it across the lawn. Anne grinned at her from her position at the end of the lawn, under a parasol.

"I doubt that," William replied, smiling. "Your aim is as terrible as you are lovely."

"Is that a challenge, my lord?" Mary said, enjoying his flirtatious tone.

William grinned as he took his turn. "Consider it so."

Mary eyed the target carefully and carefully aimed her ball. It struck William's ball and knocked it out of the field of play. Mary somehow suppressed a whoop of glee but could not contain a smug smile.

William frowned, and narrowed his eyes, and was about to take his next throw when a loud voice hailed him.

"William. There is no time for such frivolities." William and Mary turned to see his father, the Duke of Mormont storming their way across the lawns his arms folded behind his back, his face puce with rage. "Would you join me inside?"

William looked at Mary and smiled sadly. "Would you excuse me, Mary? I will return shortly."

Mary nodded silently, knowing all too well that the duke was unlikely to be overjoyed to find her playing bowls upon his lawn. She couldn't deny her disappointment that he had returned so soon, but she forced herself to remain hopeful. She tried desperately to remind herself that she was no longer the waif that William had taken pity upon. She was a young woman of means now. She had nothing to be ashamed of.

Anne got up from her place in the shade and walked towards Mary. "Is that his Grace?" she asked softly, taking Mary's arm as they walked back towards the house, up the steps, and onto the terrace.

Mary nodded. "Yes, that is the Duke of Mormont."

"I thought he was not due to return to Caldor House until later in the month?" Anne said thoughtfully.

"It would appear that he has returned home early," Mary replied a little distractedly, as she considered how the exchange between father and son might be progressing. Why would the duke be displeased? He must surely have been consulted before William offered his invitation?

But then it struck Mary. What if he had not been asked? What if William had invited her knowing his father would be gone for the duration of her visit? What if Charlotte had agreed to act as hostess, without her father's permission? She knew the duke could be a hard man, and that it was unlikely he'd be happy about his son and daughter entertaining a woman like herself. Why had she not considered that before? Had her hope and her affection for James clouded her thinking?

"I think we should collect our things," Mary said, anxiously wringing her hands as they took a seat on the terrace in the sunshine. "I am well aware that his Grace holds less than no regard for me. It might be easier for everyone if we were to arrange to return to London as swiftly as possible."

Anne gave her a sympathetic look and clasped Mary's hands. "It will work out for the best," she assured her. "Perhaps we should wait to see what Lord William and Lady Charlotte wish for us to do?"

One of the maids brought out some refreshments for them, but Mary could barely manage more than the tiniest of mouthfuls of the scones and had drunk no more than a sip of her tea when William and Charlotte emerged from the doors behind them. Charlotte looked pensive, but William smiling. Mary was unable to settle until she knew all that had passed between him and his father. "Is everything alright?" she asked nervously.

"Everything is quite alright," William assured her politely, taking a seat beside her. "I am glad to see that you did not wait to have tea."

"Mrs Churchill must have seen that our match was over and had one of the maids bring it out to us," Mary replied distractedly as Charlotte poured tea for herself and her brother. Mary looked at William quizzically. "Are you truly sure everything is alright?"

With him so close, Mary could see that his smile was tight, almost forced. "Yes. My father came home early, but he has to leave again shortly. You need not worry. Everything will be fine."

William's assurances eased Mary's concern, though his obvious forced jollity over afternoon tea and the unusual quietness of Lady Charlotte continued to nag at her, continuing to affect her appetite, and making Anne look at her with concern. Their repast was almost done when the Duke, himself, joined them on the terrace. Mary and Anne leaped to their feet and offered him deep curtseys.

"I am the Duke of Mormont, and I must apologize for not greeting you properly earlier, ladies, it was most remiss of me," he said, offering them the most perfunctory of bows. "I was not informed that I should expect guests," he added pointedly.

"Your Grace," Mary and Anne said in unison, as William stood to present them. The duke's words were almost gracious, but the same could not be said for how he spoke them. Mary could feel his disdain and wished that she could be anywhere in England rather than in front of this man who had decided he despised her without ever getting to know her.

Mary glanced in William's direction. He looked as uncomfortable as she felt, as did Charlotte. "Father, may I formally present to you Miss Mary Durand, and her companion, Miss Knorr."

"A pleasure to meet you both," he said brusquely. "Please, forgive me if I do not join you, but I have pressing matters in town I must attend to immediately, but I shall return for dinner."

"Thank you, your Grace," Mary said, her voice little more than a whisper.

"Capital. I look forward to becoming better acquainted then. Do excuse me." He turned on his heel and disappeared down the steps, then turned in the direction of the stables.

Mary sat down, her body shaking all over. She felt quite overwrought. Charlotte took her hand. "It will be quite alright," she assured Mary. "Father is never polite to anyone."

"That is certainly true," William agreed. "Think of him as a glowering black cloud on the horizon. He looks mean and acts badly, but he passes swiftly, never staying anywhere too long."

Mary was grateful to them for trying to reassure her, but she struggled to see that the Duke of Mormont would ever be a cloud that passed her over. She knew she was not of his class. She knew that William was not a man she should set her cap for. Nothing but hurt could come from that. But knowing that had not changed the way in which her heart felt. She loved William, right or wrong – and it hurt that his father could hate her so much, simply because her own father was little more than a merchant.

"Shall we continue our game?" William asked, keen to

lighten the somber mood that had come over the little party.

"William," Mary said, giving him a meaningful look. "Anne and I should leave. It would be for the best."

"Trust me," he said calmly. "Everything will be well." He offered her his arm, and Charlotte and Anne followed on behind them. Their game was a distraction, and the heated competition between the two teams, of William and Anne versus Mary and Charlotte, made them almost forget the awkwardness of the duke's arrival. But Mary continued to fret whenever she had a moment of peace. As she bathed and dressed for dinner, she had a belly full of butterflies, snakes, and all manner of other unpleasant things, making her feel nauseous and afraid.

Anne had picked out a wine-red silk gown for her to wear that night. She had been concerned when Charlotte had suggested the fabric that it might make her look pale and insipid. She had avoided strong colors, as they had a tendency to wash out her delicate complexion and blonde locks. She had been surprised to see that instead, the rich color accentuated her looks, making her golden curls seem more lustrous and her skin luminous. The gown gave her confidence, and she knew she would need that in abundance if she were to survive this night. She added ruby earrings and a matching necklace that her father had given her as a gift on his return from America. She looked very different from the girl who first graced the halls of Caldor House, starving and freezing with cold.

Perhaps the Duke had not recognized her. She did look utterly different from the skinny, grey child she had been last time she had stayed in this house. Perhaps that was why he had not been more unpleasant, earlier? Perhaps he was just being mannered, and keeping his distaste for her to himself? There were so many questions to be answered, but Mary knew she would not ever get a single one answered to her satisfaction. Polite society hid from unpleasantness behind its façade of manners and rules.

William was waiting for her in the hallway. He smiled when he saw her and Anne on the stairs. "Mary, you look lovely." He took her hand as she reached his side and kissed it gallantly.

"You say that each day. I am not inclined to believe it," she replied, his obvious pleasure at the sight of her making her feel warm inside.

"You should. I say what I mean, always. You do look lovely. As do you, Miss Knorr, that grey velvet suits you perfectly." Anne blushed and ducked her head. Mary smiled. William was always so kind to include her companion in all they did. He offered Mary his arm, as he always did. "Shall we?" Mary smiled and nodded silently as she took his lead.

As they made their way into the vast dining room, Mary couldn't help wondering aloud about all the things that had been bothering her since the Duke of Mormont's surprise arrival. "William, your father was most polite to me. I was not expecting that, to tell the truth. I had just been telling Anne that I thought we should pack and make our excuses to leave because I feared he would be so upset at my presence."

William sighed. "I did not tell Father precisely who you were."

Mary had suspected as much, but it was still a shock to hear William admit it. "You did not tell him that I was coming to stay?"

William frowned. "Mary, my father is a busy man. He forgets names, though he rarely forgets faces. He was not expected to return until long after your trip was scheduled to end. I did not see the need to cause you discomfort - or add to his ill humor by informing him of your visit. I did not expect him to return so suddenly."

"William," Mary said aghast. Her nerves had been on the raw as it was, but this news did nothing to ease her mind about the coming encounter with his Grace. "No wonder he was so angry when he arrived."

"I will make all well," William assured her. "Come what may, I will deal with whatever unpleasantries may follow. I will take full responsibility, as I should."

Mary's grip grew tighter on William's arm as they entered the dining room. Charlotte and James were already seated to the left of the table. Charlotte smiled warmly and hurried forward to greet Mary with a sisterly kiss upon the cheek and a reassuring squeeze of her hands. James greeted them more formally with a polite bow.

The duke was waiting by the mantel, a full glass of claret already in his hand. The moment they entered, he turned and gave a tight-lipped smile. "Welcome," he said as he strode towards them. Mary dropped into a deep curtsey. Her breath was so shallow and fast that she feared she might faint. She barely dared to breathe at all as his Grace took her hand, raised her up, and, patting her knuckle gently, escorted her to a seat to the right of the head of the table. William led Anne to the table and seated her beside Mary before taking the seat at the foot of the table himself.

The aroma that filled the room when they served the meal was positively intoxicating. A rich broth, made from oxtail, was brought out first. The duke looked delighted. He dipped his spoon and ate it all in a matter of moments. It was clearly a favorite dish. Its beefy richness stimulated the appetite and made Mary eager for more, despite the churning in her stomach.

⁻ But with his now empty plate, the duke was free to speak, and he wasted no time in quizzing Mary. "Tell me, Miss Durand," he said, his tone even and calm. "Your family, where are they from?"

Mary almost choked on a mouthful of the delicious broth, as he leaned back in his chair, his plate empty, and sipped his wine. Mary looked at William, then at Charlotte. Both looked as nervous as she felt. But Mary was determined not to let herself feel the shame she had from time to time in London when asked such a question. She was not ashamed of her father. In fact, quite the opposite. She was immensely proud of him and all he had achieved.

She took a deep breath, straightened her spine, and looked at the duke, her head held high. "My family is originally from Tynson, your Grace, in Leicestershire. However, my father and I now live in London, in Mayfair."

The duke nodded approvingly. All the finest people had a London address, and Mayfair was amongst the most fashionable parts of the City. "And what does your father do there," he asked. "I assume he is a merchant or some such?"

Mary knew that if she said the wrong thing that he would remember who she was. She swallowed her fear and answered carefully. "My father is an inventor, your Grace. He is currently traveling with the Duke of Compton, as the duke has been kind enough to offer Papa his patronage."

Charlotte gave her an approving look. Mary had adeptly managed to find her way through the minefield that such a question could have posed. By mentioning the Duke of Compton, she had added cachet to her father's reputation. "I see," the duke said, his expression showing grudging respect.

The main course was brought out. Large tureens of goose cassoulet appeared, and the dish was served to them at the table. It was a recipe Mary had never tried before. It was succulent and full of flavor. Mary vowed to visit the cook and get the recipe so she might pass it on to Cook when she returned home to London. Mary was sure her father would love it.

The duke watched her as she ate. Mary was careful to take tiny morsels, and to chew carefully with her mouth closed. She didn't take a sip of her wine, or water, without first being sure she had finished swallowing every bit, to ensure she didn't leave a smudge of her lips upon the glass. It was most disconcerting to be the subject of such scrutiny, but she did the best she could.

The duke drew in his breath sharply, his eyes narrowing suddenly. "It seems we have met before Miss Durand," he said, his tone icy. "I did not remember until this moment." Mary dabbed the corners of her mouth with her napkin and pushed her dish away, suddenly unable to eat another bite.

The duke did the same in a mocking parody of her. Pushing back in his seat, he stood. "William, would you join me in the study for a moment?"

Mary cringed inside but did her best to keep her expression passive. She did not wish to give this man the satisfaction of seeing her disconcerted. William looked at her, giving her a tight smile, then looked at his father and nodded. Setting his napkin aside, he stood up and bowed to them all. "Excuse us, ladies, James. I shall return forthwith."

Mary sat silently, unsure of what to do. Anne took her

hand and held it, sensing her anxiety. "Mary, it will be quite alright," Charlotte tried to assure her. Mary was not so sure, and her suspicions proved correct when the sound of raised voices echoed throughout the house. Her heart fell through the floor, knowing that she was the cause of such friction between William and his father.

Mary left her seat and walked into the hall and stood outside the thick, oak doors of the study. She could hear their exchange more clearly here, and every word was like a dagger in her heart. Charlotte tried to lead her away, but she would not go. She needed to hear every word. With a nod of understanding, Charlotte accepted that, and simply stood with her, an arm around Mary's waist. Anne took her hand, and the three women stood together, as tears pricked at the back of Mary's eyes, listening to father and son fight.

"I want them out of my house!" the duke said, his voice full of venom. "I bore her presence once at great pain. I will not do it again."

"Father, it is not what you think," William tried to interject, but the duke had no intention of listening to a word he said.

"I can see that you thought to bamboozle me. That dressing her up and teaching her some manners would change something." He paused. "William, that woman will never be seen in your company again. She is beneath you. She and her companion will leave this house with all haste and not return to it. Is that understood?"

"Father, you are being unfair," William protested. "Miss Durand may not be an aristocrat, but her character is finer than any I've ever known. She is polite and has better manners than half *The Ton*. I shall not let you berate her, when you know so little of her."

"Her own family treated her like refuse and still you want me to welcome her?" the duke retorted. "They starved her and left her for dead at the side of the road like an animal. What manner of people would so something like that, unless there is something wrong with the girl?"

"You blame her for their cruelty?" William said quietly, but his voice was full of rage. "She sought to escape an unfortunate situation. One that any person could fall into. She was left, as a child, with unscrupulous people. Why should I or anyone look down on her for that?"

"Because she is related by birth to those people?" the duke sneered.

"Father, you are not so heartless," William said aghast. "You can see for yourself that her family has risen in rank and wealth. Yet you cannot see past what was and note the beautiful, generous, and kindly woman that is before you. You were blind before Father, but surely you are deaf as well if you cannot understand why I wish her here."

Mary had heard enough. "Come, Anne," she said turning to her companion. "Let us retire." Mary straightened her spine, kissed Charlotte goodnight, and walked from the room. She did not turn to the left nor the right, and she did not look back as the argument continued. Anne held her arm as they walked up the stair together. She joined her in her room, closing them in and shutting out the din from below.

"I'm sorry, Mary," Anne said as she helped Mary to undress. "It was not fair of him to say those things. You are the kindest and sweetest person I know. Your past should not matter more than who you are inside, and what you are doing with your life now."

"But it does. To the duke and those like him it matters

a great deal," Mary replied. "We saw it all too often in London. I was a fool to think that things would ever be any different, just because I was blessed enough to meet a handful of people who didn't judge me because I was born poor."

"Like Lord William and Lady Charlotte?" Anne said. "And Captain James. They see you as you are."

Mary looked at Anne sadly. She wasn't so sure of even that anymore. "Anne, William invited me to stay at a time when he was sure that his father would not be here. He didn't even mention our stay to his father." She sank onto her bed. "The duke's return took him by surprise."

"I don't understand why that is such a problem," Anne said naively.

"You would not. You are sweet and kind and good," Mary said, caressing Anne's cheek tenderly. "We do not think as they do. But quite simply, William would not have invited us here, if he knew his father would be here. He knew it would cause nothing but trouble."

Anne's head bowed. "I see. I did not know that."

"It is alright," Mary replied with a sigh. "We shall leave this house as soon as we can. We will not impose a moment longer on those who do not wish us."

"What about Lord William, Lady Charlotte? Surely they will not want you to go?"

"William will understand. It will make things easier for him as well. I would not wish to be a burden to him. Now or ever." She smiled at Anne. "Now, we must start to pack, so we are ready to go first thing tomorrow morning."

Anne nodded. "I shall fetch your trunks and the packing velvet straight away."

CHAPTER SEVEN

When he emerged from the study, William was disappointed to learn from Charlotte that Mary had heard every word and had retired to her rooms. His father had shamed him, calling Mary such things and suggesting that she was in any way to blame for the treatment that she had suffered at the hands of her terrible aunt and uncle.

Father was belligerent, old-fashioned, and frankly wrong. But William knew all too well that it was unlikely that he would find an argument to sway his father's position. The duke was determined that Mary would not remain in his house and though it hurt William to have to retract his invitation to his beloved guest, he knew better than to challenge his father's edict.

After a long and sleepless night, William knocked on Mary's door. Miss Knorr opened it cautiously. "Good morning," he said to her kindly. "Might I speak for a moment with Miss Durand?"

Anne closed the door momentarily. William could make out her voice and Mary's, but no words. A few moments later, Mary appeared, closing the door behind her so they were standing alone in the corridor. "Good morning, my Lord," she said politely.

"Mary, I cannot tell you how sorry I am," William said anxiously. "My father is set in his ways. He is old and full of bitterness."

"You should not speak ill of your father," Mary said firmly. "He only wants what is best for you."

"Does he?" William asked, incredulous that she should be supporting his father. "He seems to want what is best for the Duchy, rather than what is best for Charlotte and myself."

"Surely they are the same thing?" Mary said. "One day, you will be the Duke of Mormont. He is holding the estate in good heart for you."

"He keeps it in good heart for his own vanity, and that alone."

William paused and looked closely at Mary. Her beautiful blue eyes were tinged with redness, and her eyelids looked a little puffy. She had clearly been crying over what she had heard, and yet was still trying to keep the peace between him and his father. It made William even more mad at his father, that the man simply refused to see how good and kind and decent Mary was.

"William, you are an earl," Mary said sadly. "I am the daughter of a man that got lucky and made something that might benefit others. I was not born to all of this – and it is incredibly hard trying to appear as if I was. I was born poor. There is no shame in that. My father has come good – and there is no shame in that, either. But I will never be an appropriate companion to someone like you."

William knew that to many of his acquaintances, her words were the truth. It was how Society maintained itself.

But William would not ever understand how an accident of birth made them inherently different. He could so easily have been born into a different family, with a different life to the one he had lived. He could have been a beggar boy on the streets or a merchant like Mary's father.

Mary was kind and good. She had worked so hard to become accomplished, to learn the skills she needed to blend into London Society, though she had not been born to that world. Her father had traveled across the world to make something of himself. He had educated himself and his daughter and had done all in his power to improve their station – and succeeded. Peter Durand was a man to be respected. He was intelligent, practical, and driven to make things better.

William had been born the son of a duke. He had done nothing to gain his title or the lands he would one day inherit. He had not proven himself in any way, other than on paper by means of his family pedigree – Father had made sure of that. He had been given no responsibilities, whilst also being expected to always do as his father bade him do. He was weak and had spent too much of his life doing as he was told for fear of the consequences. He was less than half the man that Peter Durand was. And yet, despite his weakness of character and lack of achievements, he was accepted and lauded in Society whilst Durand and Mary were not.

"William, I shall leave as soon as I can arrange for a suitable carriage for myself and Anne."

"Mary, there is no need for you to go back to London," William insisted. "Father will be gone in a day or two."

"William, I must go," Mary said, laying a cool hand on his arm. William clasped it tenderly. He never wanted to let her go.

"At least let me see if I can find somewhere for you to stay, locally, so we might continue to enjoy each other's company?"

Mary frowned. William knew he wasn't making this any easier for her, but he couldn't bear for her to leave the county entirely. He had grown accustomed to her presence. He liked spending time with her. She made such clever observations and even sitting quietly in the library reading in silence with her was a joy to him. He knew it was selfish of him, but he wanted her to be nearby.

"William, do you not think it would be better for us all if I were to just depart from your lives? You will soon forget about me if I am not here. You did before."

"That is the most ridiculous thing you have ever said." William looked at her with wide eyes. He was shocked that she could ever think such a thing. "Charlotte could never forget you. I could never forget you."

"Both of you stopped writing," Mary pointed out. "I would never have heard from either of you again, had we not met in London. In time things would be as they were then."

"That could never be," William protested. "I could not ever forget you."

"I fear that you must," Mary said simply, her eyes sad. "I am not ever going to be good enough in your father's eyes. He will not tolerate my presence in his home, and I will not cause more friction between you."

As always, she put him and everyone else in front of her own wants and needs. William had never known anyone so pure of heart, so kind and generous. Given all she had experienced as a child, she could so easily have become hardened and cold – yet she was sweet and good, and deserved none of the censure she was subject to.

William wished he knew how to change the world so that she could be happy. She deserved it more than anyone.

"At least let me find somewhere for you and Miss Knorr to stay," William begged. "Your father must have closed up the London house before his travels. Even if you send on a letter by fast rider, it will take some time to ensure the house is ready for you to return to."

Mary looked at him, as if she wanted to agree but shook her head, as if to ward away his foolish notions. "William, I know you mean well..." she started.

"Mary, you are here at my invitation. And I should have been truthful with my father. That I was not, is my fault, and mine alone. You should not have to curtail your time here in Alnerton, with Charlotte and George, because of my failings. Let me put this right?"

"Fine," Mary said, rolling her eyes as she gave in to his pleading. "But until you can arrange somewhere for us to go, Anne and I will keep to our rooms. I do not wish to anger your father further and could not bear to have him shout at Anne and make her feel small."

William nodded, understanding entirely. Mary went back into her room, leaving him alone in the corridor. It wasn't until he was halfway down the stairs, that he realized that, yet again, all her care had been for others. She did not wish to anger his father or have Anne hurt. There had been no mention of her own pain – which must have been considerable. She was a sensitive soul, and the evidence of her tears, shed in private, had been obvious to him.

Charlotte was awaiting him in the drawing-room, a pot of coffee on the table beside her. "William, how does she fare?"

"Not well, Sister," William admitted, taking the cup of

coffee she poured for him and adding heaped spoons of sugar to take away its bitter taste. "She is packed and ready to leave, would have already gone if it weren't for the need to procure transportation."

"You have convinced her to stay, have you not? If not here, then in Alnerton? We have barely got to know one another again, after all these years. I do not think I can bear to part with her so soon."

"I feel the same way, Charlotte, but where could she stay? Mrs Harris' boarding house is full, I believe and there is nowhere else."

"Why should she not come and stay with us?" Charlotte suggested. "I could send word to Mr. and Mrs. Watts. I am sure they would be delighted to welcome a guest such as Mary to stay. There is more than enough room at Watton House."

"Do you think so? It would be the perfect solution," William agreed. "I only did not suggest it, because, well, since your marriage to James, I presumed that the house was quite full enough."

Charlotte grinned. "I shall stop by in the carriage, and confirm it with Mrs. Watts straight away," she assured him. "I have to arrange for the transport of our own belongings to be returned there, as there seems little need to remain here if Mary is to leave."

William nodded and sipped at his coffee. It was hot and sweet, and it gave him a little comfort. He just wished he knew how to bring some measure of that to Mary. She had done nothing but care for others and was being treated most unkindly by his father. Charlotte stood up, kissed him on the cheek, and then left the room. He could hear her ordering the carriage in the hallway and sent up a silent prayer that Mr. and Mrs. Watts would indeed be inclined to open their home to poor Mary.

His momentary peace was shattered though, by the bellowing of his father "William, with me," he ordered as he swept out of his office and across the hallway. "We have matters to attend to."

William exhaled forcefully, set down his coffee cup, and followed the duke outside. Two horses were saddled and awaiting them at the bottom of the steps, held by the stablemaster. Father used the mounting block to mount the chestnut, leaving the grey for William. He stuck his foot in the stirrup and bounced up into the saddle.

"Where are we headed to?" he asked once he'd shortened his reins and adjusted his stirrups.

"Jem Miller notified me that there is a problem at the mill. I assured him we would go help him to find a solution. We cannot afford to have it out of action, for even a day."

"I agree," William said, as they spurred their horses to a canter. "The villagers must be able to grind their grain."

"And we must get the full profit we can from the harvest," his father reminded him.

"Of course," William muttered to himself. "The estate must always come first."

Thankfully, the duke did not hear him, the wind in their ears was too strong. But as they approached the village square, they brought the horses to a more sedate walk. "Is she gone?" his father asked him.

"No, but we are making suitable arrangements for her to do so," William said through tight lips. He longed to berate his father for the fool that he was, but even now, he did not dare. He had risked enough with his outburst last night, he would not risk a scene in public. His father would never forgive him for that.

"I want her gone," Father said firmly as if it were the last that needed to be said on the matter.

William cursed himself for a coward as they rode out the other side of the village and down the lane towards the river. The imposing mill building sat perched on its edge, its mighty water wheel not turning. Father dismounted and moved towards the wheel, looking it over with his eagle eyes. William chose to go to the mill itself, to greet Jem.

"Good day to you, Master Miller," William said, doffing his top hat.

Jem grinned and did the same with his cloth cap. "Lord Cott, it is good to see you."

"What seems to be the trouble?" William asked him, as they moved towards the wheel and William's father.

"Your Grace," Jem said with a bow. "It's the river itself," he said pointing at the still river. "All this dry weather we've had, there's not enough power in the water to drive the wheel."

"And what can we do about that?" William asked.

"We could build weirs," his father said, starting to walk upstream. "By gating the flow, we can create times of feast and famine, so to speak, and keep the wheel turning when needed, and letting it rest when it is not."

"Aye, your Grace, that'd do it," Jem agreed.

"But that would cost a lot of money, wouldn't it?" William pointed out.

"Aye, my Lord." Jem looked at his feet. All knew that Father hated to part with money unless he had to.

"Indeed, it would, William," his father agreed. "But, perhaps in this case, it may be for the best. Not only would suitable management of the river help the mill, but it could also improve the fishing. Weirs are quite remarkable things. You should read about them, my boy."

There was little William could add to the conversation. Instead, he trailed behind the miller and his father, listening to them speak. It frustrated him that, though his father insisted upon his presence for matters such as this, that his father did not ever entrust him to deal with them alone. True, in this instance he wouldn't have known what to suggest, but he didn't doubt that Jem would have given him good advice he could have taken back to Caldor House to work on.

He felt like a child in a man's body. To many, he appeared to be blessed beyond measure. An earl, heir to the Duchy of Mormont, William was the envy of all of Society. And yet, he had no power, was beholden to his father for everything, and even though he had reached his majority some years past, he had no say in his own life. He wasn't even allowed to choose his own friends - or invite them to his home without fear of his father's disapproval.

The matter dealt with, and sufficient funds promised to Jem to do what was needed, the two men rode back to Caldor House. "I keep you by my side to teach you what you will need to know when I am gone," his father said.

William took a deep breath before he reacted. "I mean no disrespect, Father, but given I have been accompanying you like this for many years, is it not time to let me try out my knowledge? Surely it would be better for us to find out any holes in my education before you are not here to correct them?"

His father chuckled. "I can see your fancy education at Cambridge wasn't wasted at least," he said wryly. "You have a way with words, my boy. Perhaps you are right. I do not give you enough freedom to make mistakes – but it is only because I do not want you to make mistakes."

"Aren't they oftentimes the way we learn our most valuable lessons?" William countered. "I know that at University I learned far more from what I got wrong, than all that I got right – though it smarted at the time to be told I was incorrect."

"Perhaps," his father said thoughtfully. "But there are some things that are too important to be left to you," he said looking up at the window of Mary's room. He frowned. William followed his gaze. Mary was looking out over the gardens, her face sad, when she saw them looking up at her, she ducked away from the window swiftly.

"Father, if you would just take some time to get to know Miss Durand..." he said but tailed off as his father turned his baleful stare William's way.

"William, trust me that this is a subject upon which I am considerably more knowledgeable than you. You will thank me one day."

"As Charlotte did?" William couldn't resist saying.

"Yes, in truth. Your sister has never denied that the match I made for her with Malcolm Tate was for the best."

William had to agree that what he said was true enough, in part, even if Charlotte had been most aggrieved to make the match at the time. She had found contentment as the Countess of Benton, and her marriage to Malcolm had produced her beloved son, George. She had been happy enough, but it didn't change the fact that their father's interference had robbed her of many years she might have been able to spend with James Watts.

"And what if I am not content to be told what to do any longer?" William asked, curious as to what his father's answer might be.

"It would depend entirely upon the matter in hand," the duke said brusquely as he dismounted and went inside the house, leaving William to take both horses round to the stables, wondering precisely which matters his father might deign to leave in his own hands, and which would be permanently dependent upon the duke.

CHAPTER EIGHT

Mary spent a quiet night in her rooms with Anne. They played cards, and Charlotte arranged for a tray to be sent up to them for their supper. It was a sad end to what had been a wonderful visit. They took to their beds early, where Mary lay, staring up at the ceiling. She had enjoyed being here, with William, Charlotte, George, and even the somewhat shy James. She had briefly been able to forget that she did not belong here.

But that sense of belonging had been ripped away from her, much as it had been at the Earl of Wycliffe's party. She was not, and never would be, accepted by those that truly mattered in Society. She was the daughter of an inventor, and no matter how successful or how wealthy he might become, how great the annual income he might bestow upon her, to *The Ton* he would always have dirt under his fingernails and calluses on his palms from the manual work he had done his entire life.

The aristocracy was not wealthy because they worked

hard. They were wealthy because they held the reins of power and controlled those that made the wealth for them. They employed overseers, managers, and bailiffs to get their hands dirty, whilst they lived in their fine homes and did very little. It had ever been thus.

The clamoring of the merchant classes, as their wealth and influence grew, to be permitted entry to their clubs and institutions could be tolerated, only so far as it served the aims of those that were in charge. The Lady Patronesses at Almack's might permit a young woman of wealth, but no title, attend their soirees, but it did not mean that the young woman would find a warm welcome there. An impoverished member of the nobility might wed a merchant's daughter to bolster his diminished coffers, but such a match was an act of desperation.

The Duke of Compton and the Duke of Mormont were unusual in that regard. Both were men who liked to be in total charge of everything around them. They did seem to work hard and wished to know and understand how they made their money, how to hold onto it, and how to increase its value. Mary respected them for that. She had no doubt that many of the impoverished lords and ladies she had met in London were that way because they had paid no heed to what they possessed and had then been surprised to find that they had frittered it away.

Mary wished things were different, but she did not blame the Duke of Mormont for his feelings towards her. He would do all he could to protect William and the inheritance that would be left to his son upon the duke's death. It was admirable, even if it meant that Mary would always be considered to be unsuitable. She accepted her place. Much as she loved William, she knew he could never be hers. But she did wish that the duke had not seemed to be so opposed to her even being friends with William and Charlotte.

Unable to sleep, she got up and moved to the window. She looked out over the grounds and wondered if she would ever be permitted to visit here again. She so loved Caldor House. She had been shown such kindness and friendship here. But she had also experienced the pain of knowing she could never fit in here, too. The duke's feelings were only a part of that pain. The greater part, by far, was that she would have to leave William, and not see so much of him – perhaps, not see him at all, once his father made a match for him.

As she stared out at the starlit sky, Mary noticed a shadowy figure walking along the pathway of the knot garden. She would know that silhouette anywhere. William was as unable to sleep as she was, or so it would seem. She smiled sadly, knowing that no matter how much she loved him, she could never have him.

As he drew closer to the house, and the blaring lamps of the wide terrace, he glanced up at her window. Mary was about to step back, as she had done earlier, but something made her stay. He stared straight at her – his expression as sad as her own. She waved to him, just the tiniest of motions, and he bowed deeply. Mary sighed and turned away. It was too painful to think what might have been, had she only been born to someone other than her own parents.

When she woke in the morning, she held that moment in the stillness of the night in her heart. Even though not a word had been spoken, it had been the most intimate moment of her entire life. She knew there would never be another man for her. She was the kind of woman that would only ever give her heart to one man – as Charlotte had. But Mary would not get the happy ending that Charlotte had been blessed with in the end – no matter how much she fought to make it otherwise.

Charlotte bustled into Mary's rooms, ordering the servants to take Mary and Anne's trunks and load them onto a cart outside. "Where are we to go?" Mary asked, as Charlotte kissed her cheek and bade her good morning.

"You are to come and stay with us at Watton House," she said firmly.

"Oh, Lady Charlotte, I could not impose upon you so. Surely, Mr. and Mrs. Watts have enough to do without adding us to their burden?"

"Nonsense," Charlotte said dismissively. "And as you see fit to call my brother William, and we are as close as sisters, I find it almost hurtful that you continue to insist upon calling me Lady Charlotte," she paused, then grinned at Mary. "And if you must be so formal, you probably should use my actual title now, Lady Benton." She paused, thinking for a moment. "Though, I am no longer Lady Benton, merely the Dowager Lady Benton, and am simply Mrs. Charlotte Watts, I suppose as James holds no title."

The two young women giggled as Anne entered the chamber. She looked perplexed. "What is it, Anne?" Mary asked.

"I am sorry, Mary, but I seem to have mislaid your ruby earrings and necklace," she said, anxiously. "I was sure I put them away carefully after dinner the other night, but I cannot find them anywhere."

Mary smiled. "Do not fret," she said kindly. "I put them in my trunk myself, just before I turned in last night.

They are quite safe." Anne breathed a sigh of relief and went back to her task of ensuring the last of their belongings were packed and ready to go.

"Anything that gets forgotten, we can arrange to have it sent over," Charlotte said as she tucked her arm through Mary's and led her downstairs and outside to where a very smart phaeton awaited them, William perched precariously upon the box, two glistening black horses in the shafts. "William has insisted he drive you to Watton," she said, giving the sporty carriage a derisory glance. "I daresay he will wish to show you a little more of the region as he drives you too fast along the lanes hereabouts."

Mary grinned. "I have never been in such a vehicle before. Does it truly go as fast as they say?"

"It does indeed," he promised her. "Now, where is Miss Knorr. I should like to whisk you away as soon as possible. I have a picnic in the hamper there," he pointed to a large wicker basket strapped tightly to the rear of the carriage, "and I thought we might stop down by the river for breakfast."

The suggestion made Mary's stomach growl. In all the chaos, she'd forgotten entirely to order a breakfast tray for herself and Anne. Her companion was probably just as hungry as she was – and was still rushing around ensuring everything was ready to go.

She emerged, following behind two footmen as they carried Mary's larger trunk to the cart. "Be careful," she told them. "Miss Durand's best gowns are in there."

"Miss Knorr," Charlotte said kindly as she pulled the girl away. "I can assure you that all your belongings will be perfectly safe in Tom and Graham's hands. They have delivered myself, George and all our possessions quite safely to all manner of places, all over the country."

Anne blushed beet red. "I'm sorry, Lady Charlotte," she said, dropping her eyes to the floor, as if she had been firmly chastised.

"Anne. Do come and see Lord William's phaeton," Mary said excitedly. "We are to take a ride in the country-side before he takes us to Watton House."

Anne blanched at the sight of the sporty carriage and William's eager expression. "How wonderful," she said, forcing a smile.

"He's even packed a breakfast for us – which is most kind of him," Mary added. "Are you ready to go?" Her companion nodded.

William jumped down from his perch and helped them both up onto the narrow bench. "It is a tight squeeze," he said. "But it is capital to fly so fast on a fine day like today."

The carriage ride was indeed fast. Mary had to hold down her bonnet as they raced along the narrow lanes of Alnerton. Anne looked quite greensick when William finally brought the horses to a halt by the banks of the river.

William helped them both down. Anne was a little wobbly on her feet, so Mary put an arm around her waist and led her to a grassy patch. William fetched the hamper and quickly spread a blanket on the ground for them to sit upon. Anne sank down gratefully. Mary sat beside her as William pulled out a bottle of lemonade. He poured some into a glass and handed it to Anne. "This might help settle you a little," he said, looking a little guilty that he'd caused her to feel so unwell.

"I'm sorry, my Lord," she said, her eyes brimmed with tears. "I should have warned you that I do not travel well at the best of times. Miss Durand can tell you; I was quite dreadful on the journey here."

"I am sorry, Anne," Mary said, feeling as guilty as William. She had completely forgotten about Anne's tendency towards sickness in her excitement about the drive with William. "I should have asked one of the maids to accompany us, or even had Charlotte and George follow on in the gig."

"I shall be quite well," Anne assured them. "As long as we do not drive quite so fast on the way back." They all laughed, and William promised to be more circumspect.

Breakfast outside, watching the river as it bubbled its way merrily through the countryside, was a delight. The cook had packed up boiled eggs, some ham, and a warm crusty loaf, fresh from the ovens. They spread it thickly with butter and some strawberry jam. The food was simple fare, but delicious. The setting could not have been more perfect. A willow tree dangled its branches over the river, and a family of otters ducked and swam in the gently moving water.

Mary felt her concerns and sadness drift away, as she turned her face up to the sun and smiled. "What are you thinking of?" William asked her softly.

"I was just thinking of how perfect this is," she said.

"I've always loved this spot," William told her, leaning back onto the blanket, propping himself up on one elbow. "I used to come here with James when we were boys. We used to fish here, and swim in the river."

"That must have been wonderful," Mary said with a sigh. "I didn't have much time for leisure pursuits when I was young. There was always so much work to be done."

"You didn't ever find a moment to play and forget your chores?" he asked.

"Not really," Mary said sadly, picking a daisy from the grass and twirling it in her fingers in front of her face. "My aunt didn't take kindly to my being idle."

"You don't often speak of your past, at least not to me. I know you spoke of it a little with Charlotte," William said gently. "You do not have to recall it if you do not want to, but I hope you know that I will gladly listen if you wish to speak of it."

"I don't talk of it often, because I prefer not to recall it," Mary said, trying to laugh. "It was not an easy time for me. My mother had passed away, and Papa had been so sure that this time he had made something that was going to change everything. I think, if he'd known what would become of me, he would never have left me at Grover House."

"I am sure he must," William agreed. "It must have been bad for you to have run away as you did, not knowing where you might go."

"My aunt was not a kind woman. She had a hard life, and she worked hard herself, as did my uncle and my cousins. But they paid me little mind unless I did something wrong. A speck of dust in the wrong place would get me a beating, if the roast was even a tiny bit burnt then I would be sent to bed without supper for a week."

"It sounds most unhappy and very lonely."

"It was," Mary admitted.

"I know it doesn't come close to your experience, but it was hard for us when our mother died, too," William said. "She was such a kind person, and somehow she seemed to soften even my father's heart. Once she was gone, there was nobody there to temper his moods. He withdrew what little affection he'd once offered us, and he buried himself in managing the estate."

"That must have been difficult, too," Mary said, reaching out and placing a hand on his. He smiled and took her hand between both of his, then tenderly pressed a kiss to first one palm and then the other. Mary knew she should pull away from him. It was a lover's kiss, a clear statement of intense feelings. It was not right that William have such feelings for her. But she couldn't bring herself to tear her hands away. It felt so good to have the warmth of his skin against the coolness of her own.

Anne coughed politely. It made Mary pull away swiftly. She must be touched in the head to have entertained such a gesture. "Perhaps we should get back now," she said, though she wished to remain here, holding William's hand and staring into his eyes for eternity.

William sighed. "Perhaps we should."

They packed up the picnic things and clambered back into the phaeton. William drove at a much more sedate pace this time and when they arrived at Watton Place Anne was smiling and not feeling unwell in the slightest. Charlotte had arrived, along with the cart, and all of Mary and Anne's things had been taken inside the pretty little manor house.

Mr. and Mrs. Watts emerged from the house as they pulled up to greet them with delighted expressions, James standing just behind them, his arm around his wife's ballooning waist. "Thank you so much for having us," Mary gushed as she jumped down and allowed Mrs. Watts to take her hands and kiss her on the cheek. They had only met once before, but Mary felt the same kindness and warmth she had then.

"Nonsense," Mrs. Watts said. "We are delighted to have you. We've not had guests in such a long time, and you will be good company for Charlotte as her pregnancy progresses."

"Thank you," Mary said, then turned to curtsey to Mr. Watts, before smiling warmly at James.

George tore out of the house suddenly, making a clip-clopping noise as if he were a horse. "Shall you take me for a ride today, Uncle?" he asked, as William lifted him up and set him upon the bench of the phaeton.

"Not today, but I shall come tomorrow and give you a riding lesson, if your Mama and Papa do not mind?" He glanced over at Charlotte and James for their approval.

"That would be very generous of Uncle William, wouldn't it," Charlotte prompted George.

"Yes, Mama," George said beaming. "Thank you, Uncle."

"You are most welcome," William said. "I shall call at two if that would suit?"

"It would be perfect, and you know it," James said with a grin. "It will also almost guarantee you an invitation to dinner."

"I should hope so, too, old man." William chuckled. "Until tomorrow," he said to them all, but his eyes lingered a moment longer than they should on Mary's face. She gave him a warm smile, though it broke her heart to see him leave.

She barely heard a word that Mrs. Watts said to her as the older woman bundled her inside Watton House and up to a well-situated bedroom at the front of the house. It looked out over the neat front garden and Mrs. Watts' beloved roses. "I hope this will suit," Mrs. Watts said kindly. "It's not quite as well-appointed as the chambers at Caldor, but it should be comfortable enough. I've put Miss

Knorr in the chamber next door, so you'll be close by one another."

"Thank you," Mary said. "I cannot thank you enough. We shan't stay long. Just until I can get word to London for the staff to open up the house there."

"You stay as long as you like," Mrs. Watts assured her. "You're most welcome."

CHAPTER NINE

Willliam was out of bed and ready for the day early. He bounded down to the breakfast room, where his father eyed him suspiciously, but didn't say a word, returning his attention to the front page of his newspaper. William helped himself to kippers and eggs from the buffet and sat down opposite his father.

"I shall need you to fetch the rents this morning," the duke said nonchalantly, without looking back up from his newspaper.

William waited for a moment, expecting his father to add that he would be accompanying him, of course, but no such clarification was forthcoming. "I should be glad to," he said with quiet pride. Perhaps his father had listened to him, at last, and was prepared to let him have some real responsibility, at last.

"You've watched me often enough," his father said, taking a bite from his plate and chewing it thoroughly. "It's time you did it alone."

William didn't want to wonder for too long about his

father's sudden change of heart. He was too glad of it – and the thought that he would see Mary this afternoon meant he could bear all manner of strange behavior from his father if need be. "I promised George I would give him a riding lesson at two o'clock, but I am sure if I set off immediately after breakfast that I can ensure that everything is done before then."

"The tenants will be in the Alnerton parish hall from ten," his father reminded him. "You should be finished with plenty of time to see George."

"He is learning fast," William said, tucking into his breakfast. "Everything I show him, he just seems to know it. He is a natural horseman, I think."

"He's got good hands," the duke said.

"Like his grandfather." William could see that his compliment had gone down well, as his father's cheeks flushed slightly, and the corners of his mouth curved almost imperceptibly into a smile. If William hadn't been watching closely, he would have missed it, for his father's expression soon returned to his more usual dour countenance. They finished their repast in companionable silence.

It was possibly one of the most pleasant meals William could recall sharing with his father. But it couldn't possibly last. As William got up to leave the table, his father spoke softly. "I'm not a fool, William."

"I'm sorry, Father, I don't take your meaning?"

"I think you do. I know you're not really going to Watton House to teach George. You're going to spend time with her."

"She has a name, Father," William said politely, determined that his father would not goad him into bad temper. "Her name is Miss Mary Durand."

"Whatever," the duke said. "I see you didn't deny it."

"It is true that I shall see Miss Durand whilst I am there, given that Mrs. Watts most kindly invited me to join them for dinner tonight, but the purpose of my visit is to continue George's lessons. You may ask Charlotte."

"I don't need to ask your sister," his father said. "I know you. I know you like that woman more than you should. I know that my warnings about your thinking yourself in love with such a person will fall on deaf ears. But I shall still say my piece."

He set his newspaper down and stood up. He looked into William's eyes. "Your Miss Durand is not good enough for you. She may be sweet and pretty, and polite and kind. But she is of weak stock. Just look at the state she was in when she first came here? Such a woman would not survive the rigors of childbirth."

"Mary has changed much since then. Her health is vastly improved," William insisted.

"One cannot change one's fundamental makeup," the duke said ominously. "But I shall not stop you from this folly. As you pointed out to me yesterday, it is only right that I give you the space you need to make a few mistakes so you might learn from them."

He left the breakfast room, disappearing into his study. William stood where he was for a moment, wondering if he'd truly heard his father admit that it was time that William be permitted to make his own mistakes. Father had certainly made clear that he still did not approve of Mary. His comment, that he thought her of inferior stock, made William shudder. It made Mary sound as if she were a cow to be sold at market. Yet his father had not forbidden William from seeing her. It was possibly the closest thing to a miracle William might ever encounter.

With a merry heart, he drove his phaeton into the village and set up his ledgers and cash box and waited for the tenants to arrive. The morning passed quickly, with only two tenants absent that quarter day. Once he'd noted every payment carefully in the ledgers, and checked the coins taken, William drove directly to the missing tenants' holdings. He knew his father would do the same. If they were in trouble, the duke would come to an arrangement with them. If they were sick, he'd fetch a physician. His father was a hard man, one who took his responsibilities very seriously – but he was a good landlord, and he took care of his tenants.

At Bob Smith's, William was surprised to find the forge unlit. The burly smith was usually hard at work at all hours. William couldn't remember a time when there hadn't been a billow of smoke pouring from his chimneys. Mrs. Smith opened the door, an anxious look on her once handsome face. It was lined with worry now, making her look haggard and tired. "Lord Cott, I'm sorry. I meant to be at the hall to pay our rents," she said nervously as she rummaged in the pocket of her apron and pulled out a small purse. "Only Bob's been sick, and I didn't dare leave him."

"Might I see him?" William asked. She nodded and led him inside. The house was basically one room downstairs, with a large fireplace, and another above much the same. Bob Smith lay on a cot by the fire, his face grey and his sturdy body diminished. "Has the doctor been to see him?"

"We couldn't afford it, with rent day due," Mrs. Smith said sadly, reaching for a damp cloth which she draped tenderly over her husband's clammy brow.

"You know my father would not hear of such a thing. Send for the doctor, immediately," he ordered. "Get Bob back up on his feet and in his forge. We'll cover Dr. Mortimer's fees."

"Thank you, my Lord," Mrs Smith said gratefully. "We don't like to take advantage. We prefer to pay our way."

"And you do," William assured her. "Your husband has served the parish well for twenty years, and don't think we don't notice all the things you do for everyone in the village, too." He left her thanking him profusely and promising to send for the doctor, but William decided it might be best to call on Dr. Mortimer himself, just to make sure.

His final call was on Jem Miller, who had also not made it to the quarter day session. William knew of his troubles at the mill, and his father had already told William to accept half-rent from the miller this quarter as it would take time to make the changes they had discussed. Jem greeted him with a bashful look. "Sorry, my Lord. I was going to come up to Caldor House, I just couldn't bear for everyone to see me ask for charity."

"This is not charity. The mill is not in use and the reason for that is not your fault. Therefore, it is worth half the rent you would usually pay. My father asked me to tell you that he will commission a specialist and will pay for the development of the weirs. He is most excited about their potential."

"Thank him for me, my Lord?" Jem said, shaking William's hand gratefully.

"I shall," William promised.

His duty done, he returned the rent box to Caldor House and told his father of his decision regarding Bob Smith. The duke nodded his assent, obviously impressed with the way William had handled matters. He quickly checked over the ledgers and saw that William had entered every figure in a clear hand and totaled the pages accordingly.

"Well done," his father said, offering unexpected praise. It had been such a simple task, given how many times he had attended quarter day with his father, but to know he had done it well, and that his father was content with his work made William flush with pride.

His heart feeling light, William rode to Watton House. Young George ran out of the house, his face alight with excitement for his riding lesson. "You came," he cried.

"I promised, did I not?" William chuckled as he dismounted and made to pick the lad up as he usually did upon their greetings. But George had clearly been learning about how to act with propriety, as he composed his features, bowed to his uncle, and held out a small hand to be shaken. Gravely, William returned his actions. George could not remain solemn for long, though, and he giggled as William shook his hand. William swept him up above his head as was more common, and the boy shrieked his pleasure.

Mrs. Watts had followed the lad outside. "Good morning, Lord William," she said bobbing a curtsey. "James is in the stables, preparing the pony for George's lesson. Let me walk you around." George ran on ahead of them, as William offered his arm to Beatrice.

"You are looking quite well," William noted. "I feared that your health might suffer from all the chaos of my sister and George taking up residence with you."

"I think it has been quite the opposite," Mrs. Watts said with a contented smile. "Having them near, hearing the happiness of young George has quite revived my spirits after my ill health previously."

The older woman still walked a little slower than

perhaps she had done before the illness she had spoken of so lightly. But William knew that it was not that long ago that they had feared that her life might be close to its end. It had been a grave concern to all who cared for her – as she had always cared for them. It was a blessing to see her so much stronger, and up and about the house and its gardens once more.

"He reminds me so much of you at his age," Mrs. Watts said as they watched George race around them. "He has so much energy."

"I was a terror, I know," William said, thinking back upon the pleasures of his worry-free childhood. Mrs. Watts had been as good as a mother to both himself and Charlotte. They had both been delighted when she had announced her intention to marry John Watts, once they were fully grown. Father hadn't been quite so delighted, though he had come around in time. Things had turned out well for the couple and they seemed very content together, which even Father could not argue with.

"No, you were a fine boy," Mrs. Watts assured him, "and have grown to be a fine man. I heard a rumor that your father entrusted quarter-day to you?"

"He did," William said with a smile. "He even praised me for how well I managed it."

"I am glad," Mrs. Watts said, "and I do hope it will mean that he might entrust you to take other decisions and undertake more responsibilities in the future."

"I do, too," William confessed. "It is frustrating to be a man of thirty, with no say over his own life." He hadn't meant it to, but a note of anger tinged his voice.

"Dear William, I understand your anger at your Father regarding his treatment of Miss Durand, but you mustn't let it consume you. He is just trying to do what he thinks best."

"He has told us that our entire lives, Mrs. Watts," William said. "But what if he is wrong?"

"If it helps any, though I cannot see how it might, I agree with you. I think he is entirely wrong, in this instance at least. Miss Durand shows all the attributes that anyone might wish for in a wife. She is quick-witted, sweet, accomplished, yet demure. And she has a fine income that would augment any family's estates."

"I see that, and you have obviously done so, too," William said, "but Father does not, and I do not see how I shall ever make him do so."

"Nor do I, but you must think of Mary," Mrs. Watts cautioned. "It is quite clear to me how fond she is of you – and you of her. If you truly think that there is no hope of ever convincing your father of her suitability – and if you intend to marry with his blessing – then you must be circumspect, my boy. Your feelings for one another will only grow stronger, the longer you leave matters."

"I know what you say is right," William admitted sadly. "I think of Mary almost every waking minute. I know that she is the woman that will always haunt my dreams and shall hold my heart until I die. Yet, though I cling to hope that my Father can be turned, I fear that my hope is doomed."

Mrs Watts turned to face him as they reached the stables. She cupped his chin in her hand as she had done when he was a boy. "You have ever been the sweetest of boys and have become the kindest of men. You deserve every happiness, especially after all you have gone through, with the loss of your dear Mama and the demands that your Father has put upon you. But you must remember that dear Miss Durand has had her fill of heartaches and troubles, too. She is stronger than you think – and though it would burn to lose you, if it were to happen then she would survive it as she has everything else." She paused, searching his face. "But, if you insist upon continuing to see her, you have to make sure that your father comes around."

William nodded. He knew she was right. It was unfair to them both to prolong their friendship if there was no hope of it reaching its inevitable climax. He knew, in his heart, that he loved Mary though he did not dare tell her so. He suspected she loved him – though she would never burden him with that knowledge. He owed it to her to make things right. If only he knew how to do so.

CHAPTER TEN

A letter arrived from London, addressed to Mary. She opened it with a heavy heart, recognizing the hand of their housekeeper, Mrs Derby. Mary slid a sharp knife under the wax seal carefully, keeping it intact and adding it to the box of seals she now kept. They were a reminder of how her life had changed. As a girl, in her aunt's home, Mary had not received anything through the post, except for on the rarest of occasions from her father. She now maintained an acquaintance via letter with a number of the young women that William had introduced her to in London, as well as receiving sporadic missives from Papa, and the regular updates from Mrs Derby regarding the upkeep of the London townhouse.

Mrs Derby's neat hand informed Mary that the town-house was ready for her return and that she had instructed a carpenter to fix a couple of broken windows in the attic rooms following a storm. Mary sighed heavily. She knew that it would be for the best if she were to return to London. There could be no hope of her affections for William being returned, and even less chance that if they were that they might ever be acted upon. She knew that his father would never permit such a match. But every day she spent here in Alnerton gave her more hope that such an impossibility might come to pass.

William called upon the Watts residence daily. He always had some excuse, to give George his riding lessons, or to deliver something of import from his father to Mr. Watts, to see his sister, or even just to bring something from the kitchens that Cook had purportedly baked for Mrs Watts or young George. Whenever he called, he always took time to see Mary whilst he was there, asking after her health, listening to her play the pianoforte, and admiring her watercolor paintings. He was often invited for luncheon, or to dine with the Watts', and Mary took a special delight in seeing him seated at the foot of the table, offering her his almost undivided attention.

Pulling out a pen and a sheet of thick paper that Mrs Watts kept Mary's writing desk stocked with, Mary sat down to write to her housekeeper. She knew she should say she was returning immediately but, as she set pen to paper, she heard the sound of hoofbeats on the gravel driveway. She peeked out of the window to see William cantering towards the house. She smiled and set aside the letter. She could respond later that afternoon. It would arrive in London not much later than if she were to send it now.

She hurried downstairs and reached the hallway as William bounded inside and pressed a kiss to Charlotte's cheek. He caught sight of her and beamed. Mary's heart felt lighter, just for seeing his handsome face. "Miss Durand, you look positively radiant," he said as he kissed the back of her hand, a gallant gesture that wasn't entirely proper, but that Mary secretly loved.

"As do you, you are positively bursting with sunshine," she remarked with a grin.

"I feel it," William admitted. "The weather is fine, and my father is entrusting me, finally, to do more about the estate, without offering strict, written instruction for every matter."

"Progress indeed," Charlotte said drily. "We can only hope you do nothing to make him withdraw such privilege."

William frowned at her. "I have no intention of doing anything to anger him," he said firmly. "I have followed at his heels long enough. I know what he would do in almost any situation – and I am not so proud as to not ask his advice should I need to."

"And finally," Charlotte teased, "my brother has grown up." They all laughed.

William turned back to Mary. "I wondered if you might be free to take a short ride into Bedford with me today?" he asked her. "I thought you might like to see the town before you must return to London."

Mary gave him a rueful look. "Ordinarily, I should have liked that very much, but I have asked Cook to prepare me some food to take to some of the Alnerton cottagers. We have also made blankets and some new dresses. There are many in need in the homes on the outskirts of the village, after last year's poor harvests."

"Then I shall join you," William said, "and shall see if there is anything further that we might do for them. I should hate to think of any Alnerton folk going without if there is anything we can do to help."

Mary beamed at him. She had seen so much hardship in her life, and it had become quite clear to her that many of William's contemporaries simply did not see it. They walked by, at best offering a meager portion of their wealth to what they deemed a worthy cause, but more often turning their noses up at the smell or complaining of the dirt. They did nothing to help those who would gladly live better lives if only they had the coin to do so.

William and Charlotte were both kind and generous – and did not seem to hold the same views that the poor were somehow undeserving of kindness and charity. They had helped her, despite her raggedy appearance, and had become her champions, despite her humble birth. His offer was not unsurprising, but she knew how busy he would be in his father's absence. To offer his time and resources was most generous.

Mr. Watts brought the carriage around to the front of the house, and Mary oversaw the loading of it with bundles of woolen blankets and cotton dresses, petticoats, shawls, linen shirts, thick trousers, and mittens and scarves that she, Anne, and Charlotte had knitted themselves. "You made all of these yourselves?" William asked.

"No, only the scarves and mittens," Mary admitted. "I asked in the village if anyone had any clothing they were thinking of discarding. Some arrived dirty, and in need of darning, but we fixed everything up, as good as new. They should do the cottagers a good turn until things improve for them."

Cook and Betsy, the maid, brought out wicker baskets filled with bread, hams, and jars of dried beans. Once everything was packed, there was no room left inside or outside the carriage. William shook his head, clearly amazed at such a bounty.

"I don't think there is room for you," William said with a grin. "Do you ride? We can follow on behind if John can take the carriage to the village for us?"

She shook her head. "And there is only Charlotte's mare trained to a side-saddle, so it would be impossible for both Anne and myself to ride anyway," she said.

"But you ride, Miss Knorr?" Anne nodded. "Then perhaps I can take you on my horse, Miss Durand, and Miss Knorr can ride Charlotte's mount?"

Mary was a little scared of horses, but she couldn't help feeling a touch of excitement at the thought of being so close to William, to be able to put her arms around his waist as they rode. She nodded cautiously. "I think that might work," she admitted.

Mr Watts began his journey to the village as they went round to the stables where Captain Watts was grooming a fine grey mare. "Good day, James," William said brightly to his old friend. "Can you saddle Sarabande ready for Miss Knorr to ride?"

James nodded and fetched the side-saddle. William quickly saddled the gentle grey mare for Anne, who mounted elegantly, despite the lack of a riding habit. William remounted his own horse and watched as Captain Watts helped Mary up behind him. "Hold tight," he warned her as the two horses walked out of the stable yard, then with the subtlest of movements eased into a trot.

Mary felt herself bumping around and wondered why anyone would choose such an uncomfortable mode of transport. "If you rise and fall with the horse it is easier on your..." William broke off before mentioning her derriere. Mary gritted her teeth and tried to emulate the motion William now exaggerated so she might see it more easily. She began to copy his movements and realized it was easier.

"Are you ready for a canter?" he asked. She nodded,

though she wasn't entirely sure that she was. William squeezed his calves against the horse's flanks once more and it obliged with an increase in speed again. With the wind in her face and the bunching muscles of the chestnut stallion beneath her, Mary clung tightly to William. It was exhilarating and frightening all at once, but in no time at all, they were slowing down once more as they reached the village.

Alnerton, was in the main, a prosperous village. But like many other villages, on the outskirts, there were smaller, less well-kempt dwellings, which were inhabited by those without permanent positions on the estate, working for the day rates set out by the Parish. Times had been tough for these people following an unusually wet summer which had left many crops rotting in the fields, and therefore less work available for them.

William brought his mount to a halt by the carriage which Mr. Watts had brought to a halt just outside the church gates, Anne did the same. Mr. Watts jumped down from the carriage and helped Anne and Mary to dismount. William did the same and then tied the reins of the horses to the back of the carriage. "Are you sure you have time to assist us?" Mary asked him as he came and took a bundle of blankets from her and set them on the stone church-yard wall nearby.

"I must confess, I make time to spend with you," William said softly. "I can catch up on anything my father might require of me later on, when I return home. When you go back to London, I shall not be able to see you – and so I make the time now."

Mary flushed with pleasure to know that, but his words reminded her that she must leave soon. Her being here had not been easy for William, she knew that. His father had made his displeasure perfectly clear and was unlikely to waver from his position – and yet, William had chosen to disobey the duke, and had continued to come and see her daily. It was generous and foolhardy – and it may serve both of them ill, as they grew fonder of one another – but Mary was glad of it, even if this short time was all she might have with William to look back upon once she returned to London.

Mary organized the items they'd brought carefully, then indicated that everyone should start to knock upon the doors of the small and rundown cottages. "Why do they let them get like this?" William mused as he and Mary walked from one home to another.

She looked at him in surprise. "They do not let them get like this. They are more often rented to them in worse condition than you see them now."

"Truly?" William said. "But surely these are houses on Duchy land, which means my father is their landlord. Yet I have never seen any of these people on quarter day."

"You will not see them because your father probably sends a bailiff to collect rents here," Mary explained. She had lived amongst people like this for much of her life. She often felt she had more in common with them than she did those whose parlors and drawing rooms she now shared. Though her aunt and uncle had owned Grover House, and ran a small dye-works, the house was not far from areas like this in Leicestershire.

"The people in these homes are often transitory," she continued. "They go from farm to farm, estate to estate in search of work. They may only stay in one village for a month or two. They take whatever housing they can get. They are considered not to belong to any one place, and so it is rare for any one Lord to consider them their concern."

"That is terrible," William said. "I shall check the ledgers when I return home to see what rents they are paying and when the estate last undertook works on these houses. I think it time we did something to improve these people's lot. If nothing else, having such eyesores so close to the village is unpleasant."

"And they bring disease closer to the village, too," Mary reminded him. "And that is far more concerning than a few broken windows and ramshackle roofs."

"You are right, of course."

Mary smiled to herself. Though he was a good man and did seem to think differently about many subjects than those of the gentry often did, William occasionally thought as so many of his class did – that poverty was something that poor people somehow brought upon themselves, that living in homes in desperate need of repair was somehow a choice.

She knew it was not the case. It took more than someone like William could ever imagine for someone poor to make something of themselves. The snobbery she had experienced in London Society was just a part of it. Her aunt and uncle had not been wealthy. They had worked hard, every single day of their lives, yet had not managed to pull themselves out of the class they had been born into – nor even into the higher echelons of the merchant classes. Their place in life had been set at the moment of their birth.

Somehow, Mary's father had clawed his way upwards. But he was so rare, and Mary knew that despite their newfound wealth, lovely home, and fine clothes, the two of them would never truly cross into the world that William lived in. However, it gladdened her that William wanted to learn, to open his eyes and see the world as it truly was. If only more of his kind were prepared to do so, nobody would ever need live in need ever again.

William knocked on the door of the next house. A bent-backed old woman opened it and glared at them. "Best to go away, Miss, my Lord," she said brusquely. "There's sickness here."

"Then it is even more important that we come inside, so we may see if there is anything we can do," Mary insisted calmly.

The woman looked at her suspiciously, then at William, and reluctantly stepped aside. "You'll do as you please," she said as Mary went inside the house.

Inside it was dark, damp, and cold. It stank of decay. There was no fire in the grate, and a man lay on a cot shivering, though he was covered with blankets. "Can you fetch some more blankets and plenty of warm clothes," she said to William who nodded. "And some firewood from the store at the Vicarage. Assure the good Reverend we will replace it."

William looked glad to escape the mean little house, and Mary couldn't blame him. The stench inside of sickness and filth was most unpleasant, but she did her best to hide how repulsed it left her and turned her attention to the man in the cot. "How long has he been sick?" she asked the elderly woman.

"Three weeks."

"And has he seen a doctor?" She knew it was a foolish question, but it had escaped her lips before she realized.

"What do you think, Miss. We barely have money for bread and firewood – and with him taken ill, there's no food at all."

"He poaches from the estate?" Mary asked.

The woman nodded. "Aye, sometimes gets a brace of

rabbits, occasionally they get a deer. It's good news for everyone when that happens." It surprised Mary that she was so open about it, but perhaps the woman sensed that Mary understood and had no desire to judge them.

William returned to find her bathing the sick man with his wife's assistance. He handed her the clothes she'd requested and set about lighting a fire in the grate. Mary dressed the man and wrapped him in clean blankets. He started to cough. The sound of it was harsh on Mary's ears, rasping through his chest and producing little relief. William handed her a clean handkerchief and she dabbed around the man's mouth, though she knew William had meant her to cover her own face with it.

"Your husband will need lots of nourishing broths," she said. "I shall have some sent down from the kitchens at Watton House," she promised. "In the meantime, there is bread and ham at the church. Someone there will give you your share. Keep a fire lit, keep him warm and clean, and use compresses to try and lower his temperature."

The woman nodded but didn't extend her thanks. Mary hadn't expected her to. The poor had their pride and accepting her charity would be sticking in the craw of this woman, no matter how much she needed it. She ushered William outside and waited until they were out of sight of the little cottage before taking a deep breath of clean, fresh air.

"They aren't grateful, as they should be, are they?" William noted as they prepared to go back to Watton House, all of their bounty now donated to those in most need.

"Why should they be grateful?" Mary asked as William offered her his hand up into the carriage. "If they were not paid so little and worked so hard, they would not need our charity."

William was quiet for a moment. "I had not thought of it that way," he admitted. "I should hate to have to ask for help from anyone. Why should they feel any different?"

Mary couldn't help thinking as Mr Watts drove her back to Watton House, that William had perhaps seen things he'd never opened his eyes to before today and had learned much. He was a good man. It would have come as a shock to him to see how these people lived. He had seen what he considered the working classes, those who toiled on his father's estates and earned a regular wage and lived in the village itself. But he had never ventured further, nor allowed himself to see the poverty on his own lands.

CHAPTER ELEVEN

Another invitation to dine at the home of the Watts family was more than welcome, though William was determined to return home and see what might be done to help the people he had met that day. If nothing else, he was sure that he would be able to find the materials that they might need to rebuild their homes – probably lying around in the many outbuildings at Caldor House that served as storage for everything from tools and timber to grain and hay. Generations of Pierces had hoarded all manner of things, in case of need someday in the future.

After they had dined well on roast beef, with a rich gravy, and a fine apple tart with thick cream, the entire family retired to the drawing-room. Anne took her usual place by the window and was soon lost in her book. He'd rarely known anyone to enjoy reading as much as she did, and to see her curled up upon the window seat, a lamp by her side, created rather a pretty tableau.

Charlotte and James sat together on the sofa, their hands clasped, opposite Mr and Mrs Watts who looked as in love and content with one another as his sister and her husband did, even after all these years. "Would you, perhaps, join me in a game of chess?" William asked Mary, indicating the board set up in front of the fire.

Mary nodded. "I should, though I haven't played much," she admitted. "Papa was trying to teach me, in London. He said he had found it a comfort on his travels, something to pass the time – especially on board ship."

"It will certainly distract a man," William said as they took their seats opposite one another. He wasn't very good at chess himself but playing with Mary gave him the opportunity to study her lovely face without anyone noticing.

As their game progressed, Mary seemed to bite at her lip more with each move. She seemed anxious about something. William wished she would confide in him. Whatever it was, there had to be something he might be able to do to help. She took his pawn with her rook, her hand shaking a little, then dropped the piece upon the floor. They both bent down to pick it up, their heads bumping lightly, their hands reaching for the piece at the same time. Mary laughed nervously as their hands touched, but she did not pull away.

William laced his fingers between hers and smiled at her. They lingered overlong, before sitting back up and reluctantly parting their hands. William knew from the flush in Mary's cheeks that she had felt the tingle of anticipation, the quickening of heart and breath as they had clasped hands, even for that briefest of moments, just as he had.

She coughed politely, clearing her throat, then turned to face Mr. and Mrs. Watts. "I am afraid I have bad news," she said sadly.

"Oh, no," Mrs. Watts said. "I know you had word from London today, your father is quite well, is he not?"

"Nothing like that," Mary said softly. "God be praised. "No, the time has come for me to take my leave of you all."

There was a stunned silence. Charlotte looked at Mrs. Watts, James to Mr. Watts, then Charlotte to James and Mr. Watts to his wife. Everyone looked sad at such news. But William was not just sad. It felt as if his heart had been ripped from his chest. He knew all too well that as soon as Mary returned to London, that he would most likely never see her again – at least, not as they had been seeing one another recently.

"I have enjoyed my time with you all, so much," Mary continued. "I cannot tell you how grateful I am, for your hospitality – and your friendship. But you are right, Mrs. Watts, I did receive word this morning, from our house-keeper. The London house has been reopened satisfactorily, so Anne and I may return."

"You do not need to go," Mrs Watts assured her, glancing at William, who she knew would not be taking the news well. She was right. But he had no right to stop her from going, though he longed to do so. He could offer her nothing. His father would not permit him to do so.

"You are welcome to stay here as long as you like," Mr Watts said as Charlotte and James both nodded their agreement. "We have gotten quite used to having you and dear Anne."

Mary gave a weary half-smile. "You are too kind, all of you. I cannot tell you how much I would like to stay..."

"So, stay," Charlotte said. "We have barely gotten to know one another again, and I long to know you better. I cannot lose my sister so soon."

Mary glanced over at Anne. "What should you like us to do, Anne?" she asked her companion.

"I must confess, I am rather enjoying it here. As you know, I find London loud and rather unpleasant much of the time – but I understand why you feel we should take our leave," she said tactfully. "I am happy to follow your lead."

Mary sighed heavily. William pleaded with his eyes, in his head he begged her to stay, to give him more time to bring his father around. He knew that it would be better for them both if Mary went, it would save them even greater heartbreak later, but he couldn't bear the thought of not seeing her every day, knowing she was just a short ride away.

Mary shrugged. "Then, I shall stay, but only for another week at most," she said, giving William a brief, sad look. "I cannot impose on you any longer and must return to my normal life sooner, rather than later."

William wanted to pull her to him, to hold her forever. He was delighted that she had chosen to stay, but it was bittersweet as he knew that their time together would be so short. He was not sure he could bear the thought of losing her. He loved her. He knew that now, and though it seemed hopeless, he refused to give up the hope that there would be a way to bring his father around, to have him see how perfect Miss Mary Durand was – and what an asset to the Duchy she would be.

As the hour grew late, William took his leave and made his way back to Caldor House. He was glad that Mary had agreed to remain in Alnerton. He had grown used to her presence here and dreaded the day she would return to London. It felt as though it would be the end of this most pleasant interlude from his more normal life. No doubt, his father would begin to pressure him to choose a suitable match. William could not leave it much longer, and it surprised him that the duke hadn't already begun to pressure him into marriage – especially given his determination to marry off Charlotte, twice.

ANOTHER FINE AND SUNNY DAY DAWNED, AND MARY and Anne decided to walk into Alnerton to purchase some ribbons and lace to trim a gown of Anne's. The road from Watton House into the village was quiet, but as they reached the village, Mary spied William's chestnut mount hitched to the post outside the bootmaker's shop. She had not expected to see William today, as he had told them that he had many errands to run and would be at the mill to meet with a gentleman who was a specialist in the construction of weirs. He had seemed quite excited about it when he'd told her about the benefits of such constructions as they'd played chess last night. It had meant little to Mary, but it had been a pleasure to see him so enthused about his work for his father – and the trust that the duke was finally putting in William.

The bell above the bootmaker's door jangled loudly as William emerged, blinking, into the sunlight. He glanced around and saw Mary and Anne. He waved and hurried over to greet them. "Good day to you, Miss Durand, Miss Knorr," he said, bowing as he always did.

"Good day to you, Lord William," Mary said.

"My Lord," Anne added as the two women bobbed curtseys.

"And what brings you both to Alnerton this morning?" William asked.

"We are to buy fripperies," Mary said with a smile. "We are going to the haberdasher's for lace and ribbons."

"Might I accompany you?" William offered gallantly, even though the shop was only on the other side of the village green.

"You would wish to coo over such things?" Mary teased.

"No, but I must go to the butcher's shop for Cook, which is next door," he admitted. "She wishes to change the leg of lamb she had requested of him for this afternoon's delivery to Caldor, to a rib of beef."

"Then we should be delighted to have you accompany us, wouldn't we, Anne?"

"Indeed," Anne said softly.

The trio walked along the street, pausing briefly at the duck pond at the southern end of the central green that made almost a square of the houses that surrounded it. There was a white swan, swimming serenely in circles. "Aren't they beautiful," she sighed, as it fluffed up its feathers, then settled back to its swimming.

"I must confess to finding them rather regal," William admitted. "I'm told that if they strike you with their wings that the force could break your arm."

"I'm not sure I have any intention of finding out the truth of such a thing," Mary said with a smile. "But I do like to watch them. I often feel a little like a duck or a swan. They look so calm and in control, yet when you peek below the surface, they are paddling like mad to just keep up with their friends."

William didn't say anything, but he gave her an odd look, as if he understood entirely, but hadn't thought of her that way at all. She smiled sadly and indicated that perhaps they should move on. Anne walked a little way ahead of them, as they made their way back onto the street.

The village was busy, with many people milling around talking, running errands, and purchasing items in the many small shops that were dotted all around the edge of the green. The ancient oak trees that marked the edge offered shade, and a place to rest for those who wished to enjoy a moment's peace. A couple of sheep grazed on the grass at the north-eastern edge, watched over by a young boy and a young woman was driving some geese towards the pond.

As they reached the haberdashery, they paused. "I should leave you now," William said, his tone a little sad.

"We shall see you tomorrow, shall we not? Charlotte said you would be taking George for another riding lesson."

"Indeed, you will," William said. "He is becoming an excellent horseman. I think he will become a neck-or-nothing rider when he's older – as long as he is not too afraid of upsetting his mother."

"Lady Charlotte would be right to be concerned about such a thing," Mary said, trying to scold him for encouraging his nephew to be so reckless – but she couldn't keep a straight face.

He bowed, as if to leave. But as he stood back upright, Mary spied his father, the duke, emerging from one of the grand homes on the green. He was accompanied by a white-haired gentleman, clad in a fine woolen jacket. Though she had met many of the villagers, his was not a familiar face. A young woman followed them out onto the step and stood quietly as the two men shook hands warmly. The young lady was fulsome and pretty, with a delicate complexion. She wore a very pretty, blue silk dress that matched her eyes, and she had the most perfect comportment. The duke gave her a deep bow, and she curtseyed to him gracefully.

They waved the duke off and went back inside. His Grace was about to get into his carriage when he spied William. He raised his arm as if to wave, but then saw Mary. He frowned and walked towards them briskly. "I thought you would be at the mill by now," he said to his son as he approached, ignoring Mary and Anne, quite rudely.

"Cook asked me to amend the weekly meat order," William said, nodding towards the butcher's shop. "Are you not going to greet Miss Durand and Miss Knorr, or do you intend to embarrass me, and them, by being so rude?"

Mary was surprised to hear William say such a thing to his father, and it seemed that the duke was, too. He looked quite taken aback, his eyes wide. "You are quite right," he said. "Ladies, please forgive my rudeness. Good day to you both."

"Your Grace," Mary and Anne said, as they dropped into deep, and respectful, curtseys.

He gave them the most perfunctory of nods, the bare minimum of politeness he could bring himself to offer, then turned back to William. "I would be glad if you would ensure you are ready to dine by six o'clock tonight," he said to his son. He pointed back towards the house he had just emerged from. "I have been doing some business with Alfred Keyes. He and his delightful daughter, Lucinda, will be dining with us."

"Of course, Father," William agreed.

"I must away," the duke said, with another curt nod, then turned and got into his carriage. He glared at them through the window as his coachman drove past them.

They stood silently for a moment, everyone feeling

awkward at what had just passed.

"Well, at least I now know why I am to be deprived of my favorite roast lamb," William said trying to lighten the mood. He looked at Mary intently. "I am sorry, Miss Durand, Miss Knorr." He looked saddened and weary. "I keep hoping he will change his opinion, but he is very stubborn."

"You need not apologize for him," Marry assured him. "I do understand. He has made his opinion of me quite clear – but he is concerned for your future, Lord William. He is your father, that is as it should be."

"You are too kind to him," William said. "I admire that you are able to be so generous when he has been anything but."

"It is not my place to try and change his feelings of me. I have met with too much blind hatred in my life. I will not let such an emotion engulf me – as it does those who let it consume them. I must forgive him, because he is someone you love, and I do not wish to create any more bad feeling."

"I wish I could be so magnanimous," Anne said, a little unexpectedly. She rarely gave her opinion on any matter. "He should be more polite, at least – especially knowing we must have seen how he was with Miss Keyes." She glanced over at the now empty doorstep and frowned. "She is no better or worse than you, Mary. Her father is a merchant, just as yours is – and yet he is somehow to be respected whilst your dear Papa is not?"

Anne had been brought up in the household of a baronet. She had been raised with the decorum expected by such men as the duke. She respected her own position in the hierarchy of Society, but she also knew the niceties required from those above her. To have riled such a mild-mannered and quiet person, as Anne Knorr, took a great deal. She was quite right, of course. But Mary could not ever say that out loud.

Mary often felt it strange that she, as someone not born to this world, was deemed as the senior member of their arrangement. As her companion, Anne was technically a servant — yet she would one day be the heir to a manor house and any child she had would inherit her father's baronetcy. The duke would not disapprove of Anne in the way he did Mary; she had no doubts about that at all.

"Miss Keyes is very pretty," Mary said, suddenly overwhelmed with jealousy as Anne's words sank in. It was true that the duke had treated Lucinda with grace and even kindness. She and her father had been offered the honor of an invitation to dine at Caldor House. Such actions spoke volumes to Mary. It showed the scant regard in which the duke held both her and her father - and showed his approval of Mr. Keyes and his pretty daughter. It meant that Lucinda was, for some reason unknown to Mary, the kind of woman he wouldn't object to, should William show an interest in her. Perhaps he was already considering a match?

"Yes, I suppose so," William agreed, a little nonchalantly. "Her father is one of the few men that my father might consider a friend."

"You have known her a long time?" Mary wished she didn't sound so anxious, but the difference between the way the duke had acted towards her and Anne, and the polite way in which he had behaved towards Miss Keyes had unsettled her more than she'd ever thought possible.

"Since she was a child. Her father purchased the house in Alnerton with my father's assistance when she was, perhaps, twelve years old. They are usually in London for the Season." He paused, his expression contemplative. "It is unusual that they are here when there are balls for Lucinda to attend and card parties to flirt with redcoats at. Perhaps Father has intentions to undertake more business with Mr. Keyes."

Mary didn't dare ask more. She longed to ask why Mr. Keyes was someone that the duke accepted into his circle, despite his lack of a title, but her father would never be offered the same consideration. She wanted to ask if William had feelings for Miss Keyes. She couldn't help wondering if the duke had plans for William, given the Keyes' invitation to dine at Caldor House that evening. It had been most rude of the duke to inform William in front of Mary and Anne, without extending the invitation to them as well. Not that Mary ever expected to be invited to Caldor House ever again, but the contradictions in the duke's behavior upset her greatly.

Suddenly, she felt utterly weary. It was all too much. She knew that William would have to marry someone suitable one day. She couldn't bear the thought of it, but she knew she had to brace herself for the eventuality. His father would never agree to a match with Mary, and William would never go against his father's wishes -at least, not to that great an extent.

Perhaps she should have left Alnerton, rather than agreeing to stay on another week. It was too hard, seeing William, growing closer to him, caring for him more and more with each passing day. "We should let you get on," she said a little sadly to William.

"I do have much to do," he admitted, taking off his top hat and bowing deeply to Anne, then took Mary's hand and kissed the back of it. "I shall see you both tomorrow."

The two women turned to enter the shop. The tiny bell above the door jangled madly as they passed inside. Mary sighed heavily. The sound seemed too loud, and almost hurt her head. She didn't recall it being so loud when she had visited the shop previously. She massaged her temples and pinned a bright smile to her face, though she felt anything but happy.

Anne went straight to the rack full of satin ribbons. For a small village store, there was a wide variety of colors and widths. Anne began to pick out those she wanted and the gentleman at the counter cut the lengths for her with his overly-large scissors and then folded them up and tucked them inside a small bag. Anne then moved to pick out some lace. She held up one type to Mary. "What do you think of this one?"

"It's lovely," Mary said as she leaned against the door frame. Her body felt peculiarly weak, and her limbs ached much more than they should from the short walk into the village. She assumed it must be the anxiety she felt every time she saw the duke and tried to shake it off.

Anne smiled and indicated how much she wanted of it and added it to her purchases. Mary rubbed at her throat. There was a tickle deep inside and a tightness in her chest concerned her. She coughed gently, to try and clear the feeling, only for it to develop into something more rasping and body-wracking. She coughed and coughed, so hard that she began to feel dizzy.

Anne looked at her, her eyes wide with concern. "Mary? Are you quite well?" she asked, dropping her ribbons and lace and grabbing for Mary, slipping an arm around her waist, as Mary's legs buckled.

"Anne, I think we should go back to Watton House, though I fear exposing Mrs. Watts to this, given how recently she has recovered from illness herself," Mary said, feeling frightened in a way she hadn't since leaving her aunt's house, all those years ago.

She knew what was wrong with her. She had all the same symptoms that she'd seen just the other day. She'd sent the physician, at her own expense, because she had seen such sickness cause devastation amongst the communities near her aunt's house as a girl. And Dr. Mortimer had confirmed to her when he came for his payment, that the gentleman who had been so sick had influenza.

"I shall see if I can find someone with a wagon, or a carriage to take us. Perhaps if I ask Lord William? He could ride to Watton House and fetch the gig?"

"No, do not trouble him," Mary said firmly as Mrs. Claythorne, the mayor's wife entered the shop.

"Miss Durand, you look quite fashed," she said, taking a step forward and peering at Mary's face.

"Merely a chill," Mary said, though she was sure it wasn't anything of the sort. "I shall be quite alright."

Mrs Claythorne did not look convinced of it either. She looked almost petrified, but she was kind enough to offer what help she could. "My carriage is just outside. "Miss Knorr, take Miss Durand home and tell my coachman to meet me back here."

Anne nodded and helped Mary back outside into the fresh air. She helped Mary into the carriage waiting on the street outside and informed the coachman of Mrs. Claythorne's instructions. He nodded and whipped the horses to a trot. Mary collapsed onto the seat, feeling cold and clammy. She felt her own brow. She was burning up. She closed her eyes, wishing her head would stop pounding and that every bump in the road didn't jar her body so much that she felt bruised.

CHAPTER TWELVE

William finished his work, and then made his way home. He had spent much of his day fuming at the rudeness his father continued to show to Miss Durand. He had no reason to be so unkind. He had quite publicly snubbed Miss Durand by telling William he had invited the Keyes' to dine, in front of Mary, yet had not extended that invitation to those present. It was an embarrassment to William – and he was fed up of having to feign ignorance of that.

He marched into the hallway and straight into his father's study. Father was sat behind his vast oak desk poring over a large, leather-bound ledger, a pair of wire-rimmed spectacles perched awkwardly on his hooked nose. He looked up at William and started to smile, then stopped when he saw William's expression. "You may not want Miss Durand in your house, and I have tried to respect that," William fumed. "But to snub her in such a manner is unforgivable."

"I did no such thing," the duke protested, but he looked guilty as if he knew he had perhaps gone too far. "I was simply informing you that we would be entertaining guests."

"No, Father. You ignored Miss Durand and Miss Knorr. I had to remind you to even address them. You gave the most perfunctory of greetings, then continued to speak to me as if they were not even there. Your behavior is unacceptable – and you have the temerity to claim that Mary is not good enough for your home. It is you that is not good enough for her."

His father had the decency to look chastened, for a moment. But it did not take him long to regain his composure. "I shall make amends, the next time I see them," he said briskly. "But you should go and get ready. Miss Keyes will be here shortly."

"Father, you do know that shoving Miss Keyes under my nose will not change my feelings for Miss Durand, don't you?" William asked, narrowing his eyes and trying to look into his father's soul. He'd been contemplating his father's motives for bringing the Keyes' back to Alnerton before the Season was done, for he was certain that was the only reason that they would be here and not in London. His father wished to tempt William away. The duke had come up with yet another of his attempts to force William to do as he wished and had delighted in being able to rub Mary's nose in it as he did so.

"I am well aware of Miss Keyes' charms," William said, forcing himself to remain calm. "I have known her for many years, and though I like her, she cannot hold a candle to my feelings for Miss Durand. I do not know what you hope to achieve by this."

"William," the duke said with a heavy sigh, removing his spectacles and setting them carefully on his desk. "You must take a wife soon. You cannot delay any longer. I am not getting any younger, and it would bring me peace to know that the Duchy is in good hands and that my descendants will continue to hold it."

"And I am not to choose my own wife?"

"I have given you years to make your own choice," his father said, standing up and moving around the desk. He tried to keep his expression calm, but William could hear the notes of exasperation in his father's voice. "Until very recently, Miss Keyes seemed to be your choice. I do not understand why you should have changed your mind."

"Changed my mind?" William asked. "You make it sound as if I ordered chops for supper and then on a whim decided to have eggs instead."

"Well, can you forgive me for thinking so, when you have switched your affections in so short a time?" his father asked.

"I never held Miss Keyes to be anything more than a friend," William said, biting his tongue. "And even if I did, I am permitted to make up my own mind who I wish to marry, or not marry."

His father frowned at him, making William feel as though he was a boy of ten and not a man of thirty. "If you will not choose a wife, then I must do it for you."

"What if I have made my choice?" William said, thinking of Mary.

"If you have chosen a suitable woman, then I will be delighted," the duke said. "But if it is *that* woman, then that will only happen over my dead body."

"What makes Miss Keyes suitable, but not Miss Durand?" William asked boldly. "Mr. Keyes is a merchant, has made his money in the East Indies, transporting spices. He is no better than Peter Durand."

"You know very well that Mr Keyes mother was the

daughter of Lord Grayson. Keyes was brought up in Society and has never known anything else. He has wealth and influence – and good blood, even if his family fell on hard times and needed to marry into the merchant classes. Keyes has turned that family's fortunes around – as he has his own."

"So, it was quite alright for the late Mrs. Keyes to marry a merchant, as it was for Charlotte to marry one, before she put her foot down and married James?" He arched his eyebrows and stared at his father. Could he truly not hear how incongruous his arguments were?

"I don't understand your reticence," the duke protested, ignoring William's questions. "You seemed to have every intention of proposing to Miss Keyes before you became reacquainted with Miss Durand. She is sweet, kind, generous, and very pretty –all of the virtues you assure me that Miss Durand possesses."

"That is perhaps true," William conceded. He had indeed considered proposing to Lucinda Keyes. She had the upbringing and connections within Society to make a fine duchess one day. But though he liked her and could have settled with her had he not met Mary in London, now he had, William knew he could never let either himself or Lucinda settle for second-best.

"You've not spent any time with her in months. Perhaps tonight will remind you of her many virtues," his father said, his tone encouraging. "Perhaps it will rekindle what was once there."

"I will be polite. I will be charming," William assured his father. "But I will not ask for her hand, tonight or ever."

He stormed from the chamber and up to his rooms. His valet had laid out clean clothes and the maids were pouring buckets of hot water into a copper tub by the bath. He took off his jacket and threw it over a nearby chair, kicked off his boots, and unfastened his cravat as he stared out over the grounds of Caldor House. His father was infuriating.

William looked over towards Watton House. He couldn't quite see it from here as a wood lay between them, but knowing Mary was still so close by made William feel stronger. He had never dared to speak to his father as he had just done, before meeting her. His father was learning that there was more to William than he'd perhaps given credit for. William knew his father thought him a failure. He lacked the duke's single-mindedness and hadn't the necessary fire that his father thought the mark of a man.

But, until now, there had never been anything William wanted enough to fight for it. He had been happy to live his life the way his father had mapped it out – or if not happy, he had not seen any reason to live it any other way. But Mary had changed William. She had woken him up from his slumber. He had been content to just potter along in life, to do his father's bidding. He had accepted that he would never get to choose what he wanted for himself and so had made the most of what was open to him.

But that wasn't enough anymore.

Now he wanted it all. He wanted Mary's love. He wanted her to be his wife. But he also still wanted his father's love and respect. He knew that if he chose one, he would lose the other. It was an impossible choice – or, it should have been. But William knew which he would choose – if his father forced him to make it. He would take Mary, love, and happiness over his father, respect, and duty every day of the week.

But that day had not yet come where he had to make the final decision. William still held out hope that he could convince his father that Mary was the right wife for him, so, dutifully, he bathed and dressed and went down to greet their guests when they arrived. He escorted Miss Keyes into the dining room, and he made polite small talk with her, her companion, Hannah Kingsley, and her father throughout. He showed interest in Miss Keyes' painting and asked her to accompany him on the pianoforte after dinner. She sang beautifully, and it helped to pass the time until she and her father would depart.

The duke and Mr. Keyes stayed at the dining table, talking business as they drank port and smoked cigars. Miss Kingsley sat on the sofa by the fire with her embroidery as he and Miss Keyes enjoyed their duets. As William tried to find the sheet music for a song that he knew Lucinda liked, she sank onto the piano bench beside him. "I have not seen you in a long time," she said a little sadly.

"I am sorry, I have been very busy," William said, sitting up having found the music and placing it on the stand.

"Might you permit me to make an observation, Lord William?" she asked, cocking her lovely head to one side.

"Of course," William said, suspecting what might be coming next. Lucinda Keyes was an intelligent woman. She had sharp eyes that didn't miss a thing. She would have seen that he had not hurried to greet her whilst in the village earlier that day. She would also have been aware that he had not engaged in conversation with her in the manner that he used to, over dinner.

"You seem distracted," she said. "And I suspect that it might have something to do with the rather lovely lady I saw you with earlier?" She arched a single eyebrow and grinned at him. William was, as always, impressed by her ability to see right to the heart of a situation – and not to take what others might deem as rejection personally.

William smiled at her. "As ever, you see all," he said wryly.

"She is very pretty, and I am quite jealous of the way she holds herself. Such delightful comportment."

"She might say the same of you," William assured her.

"But we are not talking of me, are we, Lord William?" Miss Keyes said with a grin. "Have you finally fallen in love?"

"I believe I have," William confessed. "And I am sorry. I know that I may have raised your hopes of a match between us, but I could not now condemn either of us to a loveless match."

Lucinda laid a hand over his, where it sat on the keys of the piano. "Dear William, I think of you as a brother. I should have been delighted to become the Duchess of Mormont, someday – but you know that you are not breaking my heart with this news."

"I am so glad," William said, relieved. "Is there someone for you? Have you met someone in London?"

"I did. But Father wanted us to come here, before I accept his proposal. He felt that there was an unspoken agreement between us – and he did not wish to offend your father."

"Too many people think that way," William said drily. "It has given the old man a sense of power over all around him." Miss Keyes gave him a quizzical look. "Father disapproves of Miss Durand."

"Ah," Lucinda said knowingly. "Then I wish you the very best of luck, dear William – but I do hope you will not mind if I when I take my leave of Alnerton and return to London, that I shall be accepting Captain DeWitt's proposal?"

"Of course, I do not," William assured her. "I wish you both much happiness. DeWitt is a very good man. I can now say that he is most certainly one of the luckiest I have ever known."

William smiled and began to play. Lucinda sang and they laughed together as their fathers glanced through the doors between the drawing-room and the dining room and smiled indulgently at them. "Little do they know," Lucinda said between the verse and the chorus.

"I shall rather enjoy telling Father that you have already set me aside," William joked. "You heartless flirt."

CHAPTER THIRTEEN

A lamp was still burning on her bedside, though it was dark when Mary woke, shivering. Her mouth felt as dry as straw and she had a fierce thirst, more so than she could ever remember having. She did not recall getting here from Alnerton, wherever here might be. The room seemed familiar, but her brain would not think clearly enough to be sure. She thought she remembered insisting that Anne should not ask William for his help, though in her delirium she wasn't even sure who either Anne or William might be.

Every muscle ached. She tried to pull herself up in the bed. Her limbs felt like lead. Breathless and exhausted, Mary reached for the pitcher of water that someone, probably Betsy, had left by her bed, clasping her hand around the handle. She went to lift it, but it was too heavy. She shifted her position a little and tried again, this time with both hands. She managed to raise it a few inches above the table, but before she could tilt it to pour some of the clear, cool liquid into the glass, it slipped from her fingers and smashed onto the floor.

A young woman burst into the room her eyes wide. "Oh, Mary, why didn't you call," she said, fetching some cloths from where they sat in a pile on the top of the chest of drawers and rushing to the side of the bed and dropping to her knees to mop up the spilled water and pick up the broken pieces.

"I didn't want to be any trouble," Mary said, knowing even as she said it that it was idiotic. "I know you, don't I?"

"Oh," the girl said, looking afraid. "It's me. It's Anne. I've been your companion for some years now. Surely you remember me?"

"Yes, yes," Mary said. "Of course, I do." But she wasn't entirely sure if she did or not. The young woman who said she was Anne did seem vaguely familiar, but Mary couldn't remember. Her mind was a jumble of words and nonsense, and images that made no sense to her.

"I feel so weak," Mary said, sinking back against her pillows, tears pouring down her cheeks. "And my throat is as dry as sand." She glanced around the room, and noted a bowl of cold water, with a couple of linen compresses draped over its side sat on the table beside the bed. One of the chairs that was usually by the window was now right beside the bed. Clearly, someone had been here mopping her brow. She felt terribly guilty for causing such trouble.

"Mrs Watts has sent for Dr. Mortimer," Anne assured her. "He will be here first thing. He's attending to a birth in the village tonight."

She spoke as if Mary should know who Mrs Watts and Dr Mortimer were, but Mary didn't remember them, either. "I do not need a doctor," Mary insisted, trying to sit back up again. She swung her legs over the side of the bed and tried to stand up.

"Mary, lie down. You aren't well. Stop being so brave, let us care for you," Anne begged, dropping the sodden rags and pieces of broken china and jumping to her feet, just in time to catch Mary before she collapsed onto the floor.

"My legs feel like they are made of blancmange," Mary said through chattering teeth as Anne helped her back into bed.

"Which is why you need to stay put," Anne said, her tone reminiscent of a schoolmistress. Mary did as she was told.

As Anne pulled the blankets up over Mary's shivering body, she put a cool hand to Mary's forehead, sighed heavily. She dipped one of the cloths into the bowl and started to mop Mary's brow, cheeks, and neck. The cold compress was soothing, and Mary closed her eyes a little and sank back into sleep.

When she awoke, a man and an older woman stood at the end of the bed. Mary tried to rack her brains to remember them. She recalled the girl, Anne, talking of Dr. Mortimer and Mrs. Watts. Perhaps this was them? Her head felt even more hazy than she had done before and drifted in and out of consciousness as they spoke. What she heard should have frightened her, but she didn't have the energy to mind.

"She has influenza, and it has led to pneumonia in her lungs," Dr. Mortimer was saying. "There seems to have been an outbreak of something similar amongst the cottagers, on the outskirts of the village."

"She was there, offering charity, just the other day."

He nodded. "I know, she sent me to see one of them, and paid for his treatment."

"She is a kind woman, perhaps too much so for her

own good," Mrs. Watts said sadly. "How does he, the cottager?"

"Sadly, he passed away. This kind of infection is not easily fought – especially amongst those who aren't strong."

"You think Mary will recover?" Mrs. Watts asked, her anxiety and concern clear in her quavering voice.

The doctor drew in a breath sharply. "I cannot say," he said cautiously. "She is much stronger now than she was when I first met her. This would have been the end of her then. I can offer you laudanum for any pain when she wakes. She will need plenty of good, warm broths to keep up her strength – if you can get them into her. If you can give her cold baths, and use compresses to try and break her fever, then perhaps..." he tailed off.

Their voices drifted further and further away. Mary tried to move her head. It felt so heavy and hurt so much. She felt someone's arm slip under her shoulders and raise her up. A glass was pressed to her lips and cool water poured slowly into her mouth. She tried to drink, but her throat was swollen and dry and much of the liquid spilled down her chin.

"We should send for William," she heard someone say. "He'd want to know."

"No," she protested, as loudly as she could, but her voice seemed to just echo in her head. She wasn't even sure if she'd managed to say it out loud. "Don't send for him. He'd only worry."

PROGRESS ON THE WEIR WAS HAPPENING AT PACE. William and his father rode to the mill to meet with the man who had come to consult on the project. Alan Marston was a very knowledgeable man and explained every aspect of the construction to them in great detail. They pored over the plans and looked over the site that Marston suggested would be the best place for the weir.

They all turned at the sound of hoofbeats behind them. James Watts raced into view. "William, you need to come, now," he demanded.

William moved towards him, surprised that James hadn't dismounted. "What is it?" he asked, his heart rate rising.

"It's Mary, she's sick," James said. "She has influenza."

"That cottager," William murmured. "He coughed on her the other day. She didn't seem concerned by it at all. I should never have let her go anywhere near him."

"She's very sick," James said urgently. "She has developed pneumonia on her lungs. Dr. Mortimer does not know if she'll..." he tailed off, unable to bring himself to say the words.

William felt all of the blood drain from his head. He knew he must have gone pale as a sheet. The thought that he might lose Mary now, was almost too much to bear. He rushed towards his horse and unhitched it, fumbling with the tough leather reins, before mounting up. "Then we'd better go, now," he said. The two men thundered away, leaving the duke walking towards the spot where they had been, demanding an explanation that would have to wait.

By the time he arrived at Watton House, William had convinced himself that he was already too late. He burst into the house and raced up the stairs to the guest bedroom, where Mary was lying, Anne mopping her brow. "How is she?" he demanded, half expecting someone to tell him she was already dead.

"Her fever has yet to break," Anne said anxiously. "She has not regained consciousness since the early hours. It seemed to come on so suddenly, but she must have been feeling bad for days."

William paced up and down the chamber. He had never felt so impotent and useless in his entire life. The woman he adored might die without ever knowing how much he loved her. Mrs. Watts appeared in the doorway. "You shouldn't be here," he said to her, thinking of how unwell she herself had been not that long ago.

"She is under my roof," Mrs. Watts said firmly. "And as long as she is, I shall ensure she is taken care of."

"She shouldn't be here," William said. "It's not safe for you."

"Where else should she be?" Mrs. Watts asked. "I won't send her back to London to be cared for by servants. She'd never make the journey, for a start."

"She should come back to Caldor," William said decisively. He did not intend to let Mary out of his sight until she was well. "I shall fetch the carriage immediately."

"William, your father will never permit it," Mrs. Watts said, looking as concerned for him as she was for Mary. William reached out and squeezed her arm.

"I don't intend to give him a choice," he said through gritted teeth. Mary needed him and he would not let his father get in the way of that. He hadn't before, and he wouldn't now. William would walk through fire to make sure Mary was safe – even if that meant standing up to his father. "Have her ready to go as soon as I return."

Not waiting to hear further arguments, William ran out of the house and galloped through the woods to Caldor House. His father had returned from the mill, and was in his study, as usual. William strode in, his face set in with a determined look. "Miss Durand is sick," he stated baldly. "She will be returning to Caldor shortly. I shall be instructing Mrs. Churchill to prepare suitable rooms for her, and I will hire a nurse from the village to care for her."

William's directness seemed to take his father by surprise. "What is her sickness to do with us?" the duke said, but his voice wasn't as sure as it normally was.

"She got sick providing care and charity to those we should have been caring for, ourselves," William said, his tone firm. "You pride yourself upon being a good landlord, taking care of all who work our land. But we have been neglecting the poorest of our workers when we should have been treating them as we do our other tenants. We need to provide the cottagers with better housing and more stable work. They are as much a part of Mormont as you and I."

The duke looked stunned. "They are itinerant, they are not our responsibility," he protested.

William scowled at the easy excuse as it fell from his father's lips. "They are itinerant because they have to go to where they can find work. But they were born and bred on our land. They pay rent to our bailiffs. They get sick because they live in such squalor. We protect the villagers and ourselves by taking better care of them."

The duke looked thoughtful for a moment, then nodded. "You are right," he said calmly. William stared at him, unsure if he had heard his father correctly. "I shall make arrangements."

William stalked from the room, too concerned about Mary to bask in his unexpected success. He went below stairs in search of the housekeeper to inform her of Mary's imminent arrival. She assured him that she would have a room ready, and would send for her cousin, who was a nurse, to come from the village immediately. "And send for Dr. Mortimer, too," William said. "I want him to check Mary over again."

His heart pounding so loud, he feared others might hear it, too, William headed out of the back door and made his way to the stables. "I need the landau made ready, immediately," he ordered the stable master. "There is no time to lose."

With a click of the stable master's fingers, a number of stable lads appeared from inside the stalls. Without being told, they seemed to know that William needed them to hurry. They raced to the large barn and rolled out the heavy, but roomy landau, as the stablemaster ran to fetch the tack for the carriage horses. The coachman led the horses from their stalls, and the two men put the harnesses on and then led them into the shafts and made them fast.

William jumped up onto the bench and took the reins from the coachman. "Do you wish me to drive you, my Lord?" he asked.

"No, I shall go alone," William said, flicking the whip and clicking his tongue to the horses. It would be better for everyone if they kept as many people away from Mary as they could. It would not do to have half the household falling sick all at once. Mary was enough for him to worry about right now.

Upon arrival at Watton House, he found that James and John Watts had managed to bring Mary downstairs on a makeshift stretcher. They'd bound a blanket to two long poles, and though it didn't exactly look comfortable, it certainly made moving their patient easier.

Anne was still by Mary's side, sponging the sweat from her brow, her own forehead furrowed with concern. Mrs.

Watts hovered nearby, looking agitated that her guest was to be removed, and that nobody would permit her to help. William embraced her, something he had not done since he was a boy. "We will ensure she has the best care. Mrs. Churchill has sent for her cousin to nurse her, and Anne will be by her side, no doubt, every hour. But I will not risk losing her, and you, my dear Mrs. Watts."

John Watts moved to his wife's side. "He is right, Beatrice. Your health is not what it was, and I am not ready to lose you."

She nodded and wiped away tears with a lace-trimmed handkerchief. "You will let us know, every day, how she fares?"

William forced a smile. "Of course, I shall," he assured her, giving her arm a gentle squeeze before taking the opposite end of the stretcher to James and carrying Mary to the landau. The wide benches of the comfortable old carriage made it possible for her to remain lying down, once they had transferred her carefully from the stretcher. John carried a trunk, that Anne had hastily packed, and slid it onto the floor of the carriage. Anne perched on top of it, wrapping Mary with more blankets, as William drove them back to Caldor House, where Mary was installed in the rooms that she had so recently vacated.

As William looked at her lying in the bed, he was taken back to the first time he'd brought Mary here, three years ago. She had looked much the same. Pale and feverish, so weak. Yet he knew now just how strong she was. If anyone could survive influenza it was Mary. She would fight. He knew that. He just prayed that she would win.

CHAPTER FOURTEEN

Mrs. Churchill was waiting for William in the hallway outside Mary's room. A plump, but kindly looking woman stood at her side. "My Lord," Mrs. Churchill said, "this is my cousin, Mrs. Alison Grey. She is a fine nurse."

Mrs. Grey bobbed a curtsey. "My Lord, I shall be honored to serve your family as long as you have need of me."

"Your husband and children will not mind your being here, all day and all night?" William asked gently, he was glad of the woman's help – but he would not risk anyone's health that had those that needed them.

"My children are grown and have families of their own, and my husband passed away a year ago. I shall be glad of the company," Mrs. Grey admitted. "I have the constitution of an ox," she said, as if reading his mind. "I've taken care of the sick for more years than I can count and have never had a day's sick in my life."

William gave her a wan smile. She was just what was

needed. "Mrs. Churchill will show you where everything is. Did Dr. Mortimer come with you?"

"No, my Lord," Mrs. Grey said. "He wasn't home, but I left a message at his lodgings." William nodded and headed down the stairs. He'd fetch the doctor himself. He wasn't prepared to wait. If there was anything more that could be done, William needed to know it was being done.

His father caught him at the door. "You are not responsible for this woman," he said, his eyes flashing angrily. He was clearly not enjoying being gainsaid in his own home.

"I am, Father. I invited her to Alnerton. It is because of me that she is here at all. She could have been safe in London. Instead, I allowed you to let me turn her away. If she had been here, she might never have gone to that part of the village. She might never have taken ill – so I will take care of her until she is well."

"I will not have her here," his father insisted, his face puce with rage.

"Yes, you will," William said. "Because this is as much your fault as it is mine. How do you think the Duke of Compton will react, should he find out that you are in part responsible for the death of the daughter of his partner in business? He will not be best pleased."

"I will disown you, cut you from my will – will bestow everything upon George."

"You think I care about all this," William gestured angrily at the house, the paintings, and the estate beyond the door. "That is what you care about. I will gladly live without all of it if it means I can be with Mary Durand." His father looked at him aghast. "You do not understand that, do you?" William said coldly. "That there are those that put people ahead of property."

"If you truly feel that way, then I want you and your beloved Miss Durand gone from here by tonight."

William just laughed. "Father. I shall leave this place when Mary is well, and not before. But take heart, we shall go – together. We will go to London, and I will beg Mary's father to give me a position and Mary's hand. I doubt we will receive the censure from him that we have received from you."

Having finally said his piece, William stormed from the house. He felt such a peculiar mixture of things as he rode at breakneck speed to the village to fetch Dr. Mortimer. Elation, that he had finally stood up to his father. Dismay, that his father had reacted the way he had. Fearless, because he had finally brought about his own freedom. And so afraid, that he might lose Mary before he could tell her all about it and tell her how much he loved her.

William had never really been a neck-or-nothing rider, though he did love to ride and drive fast. He was determined to return as soon as possible, so today he drove his mount faster than he ever had before. Riding so fast was the closest he might ever come to flying. He took the hedges and gates between Caldor and Alnerton, as if he were riding a race, and once he had seen Dr. Mortimer into his gig, William raced home to Mary's side.

He sat quietly in the chair beside her, holding her hand, willing her to come back to him. "You must get well, darling Mary, for I cannot live without you. I will not live without you" he vowed. "You are my everything. I love you, and I intend to marry you. So, you must get well."

At William's urging, Anne took a nap on the chaise longue at the end of the bed, as Mrs. Grey bustled around, ensuring she had a plentiful supply of clean linens, hot and cold water, and the laudanum that would ease Mary's pain

– if she woke and needed it. William watched Anne's breathing steady, and marveled at Mrs. Grey as she worked, holding tight to Mary's hand. He admired her efficient movements and determination for everything to be orderly.

But his attention, mostly, remained fixed upon Mary's pale face. He had seen her like this before, her hair lank and lifeless, grey circles around her eyes – and he had been afraid they might lose her then. Back then he had not cared for her, not as he did now. She had been a stranger, a waif he had found in a ditch by the side of the road. It had been easy to leave her care to others. Now, he could not bear to leave her side, in case she slipped away from him when he wasn't there. He had never been more afraid of losing anything in his life.

Days and days passed. Mary's fever showed no signs of abating. Anne and Mrs. Grey took it in turns to watch over Mary, as William got under their feet, refusing to let go his hold on Mary's hand. He read to her, hoping that her favorite books might rouse her, but nothing seemed to reach her.

He dozed in the chair beside her and ate at her bedside. He knew that the entire household was concerned for his health, that he might succumb to the influenza, as Mary had. But he refused to listen to any of them, when they insisted that he take a rest, got some sleep in his own bed, or went outside for a walk in the fresh air.

And he was rewarded when after the longest week of his life, Mary's fever finally broke. She murmured a little as Anne bathed her forehead, and her eyes flickered open. "Wh.wh.where…" her voice was husky and it was clear that it was difficult for her to speak.

"Shhh," Anne said kindly. "Don't talk. You've had the influenza, and have been very, very sick. But you're going to get better now." Mary looked up at them with tired, bloodshot eyes, then closed them and slept peacefully. Anne and William looked at each other, tears in their eyes and smiles on their lips. Mary was coming back to them, after all.

⚜

MARY'S RECOVERY WAS SLOW. IT TOOK A WEEK BEFORE she could even manage to sit up in bed and feed herself, and another week after that before she was able to get up and sit in a chair by the window. But once she had passed that milestone, it seemed that her recovery picked up pace. She was soon able to go downstairs and sit in the music room, where William would play songs for her on the pianoforte and read to her from her favorite books.

Almost every day, Cook would send up little treats to tempt her tastebuds, as her sense of smell and taste seemed to have deserted her, and she still found it difficult to eat more than the tiniest of portions. Anne coaxed her gently, but each day her appetite improved.

She marveled that William was able to spend so much time by her side. His father had always been so demanding of his time – yet, now, it seemed as if William had nothing of import to do. If Mary was awake, he was at her side. He held her hand when they sat together on the sofa and would help her to make her way up and down the stairs, letting her lean as heavily on him as she needed to. He made her feel so safe, and so very loved.

Mrs. Churchill came into the music room, carrying a small silver salver. Upon it was a letter, with a fat wax seal.

She proffered the salver to Mary, who took the letter and immediately recognized her father's disordered scrawl. She opened it carefully and kept the seal, as she always did. She smiled to see that his business in America with the Duke of Compton had concluded most satisfactorily and that he was on his way home.

"Papa says he will be with us, here at Caldor House, on the fourteenth," she remarked. "He shall come straight here from the boat and will take us back to London, Anne."

Mary couldn't help feeling a little sad at the thought of leaving Alnerton, even though she knew nothing had really changed. William's father may not have interfered with her time with William in recent weeks, but now she was well again, she did not doubt that the duke would demand more of William's time, once more.

William squeezed her hand. "Then he will be with us tomorrow," he said, his eyes filming with tears.

"Goodness, is it already so far into the month?" Mary said, looking to Anne to confirm what William had said. She nodded. "Oh, my."

Unbidden, tears began to well in her eyes, falling onto her cheeks. "Oh, dearest Mary, do not cry," he said, putting an arm around her shoulders and pulling her to him. It was not right or proper, but Mary couldn't think of anywhere she would rather be than in his arms. She sobbed, knowing that this would be the first and only time it might ever happen.

"I thought we might have more time together," she admitted between sobs.

"As did I," he said, reaching to wipe her tears with his thumb. "But it is not the end."

"It is not?" Mary asked, looking up at him. "But your father..."

"Has already told me not to darken his door ever again, because I chose you over him and the Duchy. I said I would go, once you were well enough to leave, too."

"You did... what?" Mary asked, aghast. She had never wanted it to come to this. "William, you mustn't. I know that the way I feel for you cannot ever be returned, that you have your duty to perform – and that your father will never accept me."

"Mary, I love you. How could I turn my back on that?" William asked her simply.

"But you mustn't," she said, the tears flooding down her face once more. "I won't let you."

"Mary, it is not up to us any longer. My father is a stubborn man. He will not change his mind. He has chosen to have me written out of his will and to switch the entail to Charlotte's son, George. And I am not sorry for it – or at least I won't be, if you will tell me that you feel the same way about me, too?"

"Oh, William, you know I do. I have loved you from the very first, when you saved me from death."

William beamed. "Then it is settled. I shall travel with you, and your father, to London. I shall ask Wycliffe if he might put me up until I can find suitable lodgings – and I shall have to do what I can to find a position."

Mary was both elated and worried, all at once. She was delighted that William loved her, as she loved him. But she couldn't help being concerned that he might regret giving up everything he had ever known to be with her. What if he was unable to find a suitable position? What if his friends shunned him for his choice? What if loving her and giving up everything to be with her, made him as bitter as marrying her uncle had made Aunt Jane?

"I cannot ask that of you," she said. "I will not be the one to take you from your family and your inheritance."

"You only take me from Father and the Duchy. Charlotte and James would never forsake me, nor would John and Beatrice Watts. All I lose is a fortune. But I have spent a lifetime learning of business and investments at my father's right hand. Something I have learned will be of use to me, I have no doubt. I am rather excited at the thought of making something of myself – rather than having everything handed to me upon a silver platter." He chuckled, but his voice was strained. Mary prayed he would not ever regret his choice. She knew that she would do everything in her power to be sure he did not.

CHAPTER FIFTEEN

Once he had seen Mary back to her bedchamber, so she might oversee the packing of her things, William sought out his father in his study. His father looked surprised to see him, but he continued to make entries into the ledger on the desk in front of him as if William's visit was an inconvenience he could do without.

"I'll not stop long," William said briskly. "But I wanted to inform you that Peter Durand will be calling upon us tomorrow. He will be taking Miss Durand and Miss Knorr, back to London with him. You will not have to put up with their presence in your house any longer." He turned on his heel and made to leave.

"And what about you, William?" the duke asked, just as William was about to leave.

William turned. "I thought we had already agreed on that," he said tartly. "You told me I would not be welcome here if I chose Miss Durand."

"I did," the duke said, nodding his head.

"Miss Durand has informed me that she shares my

feelings," William said proudly. "Therefore, as soon as Mr. Durand arrives, I shall be asking him for his daughter's hand in marriage. I shall return to London with them and will never darken your door again."

His father stood and strode towards him. "I had hoped you might have seen some sense," he said, his anger icy cold. "You are not thinking straight. What man would want you, a penniless aristocrat, for his daughter?"

"Father, Miss Durand and her father do not view the world as you do," William retorted. "They are good people. They care for one another. Mr. Durand is a decent man, who has worked hard to make something of himself. He has more decency than anyone I've ever met – especially amongst those who merely inherited their wealth. He will understand my desire to find my own place in the world. He will probably even be kind enough to help me do so – unlike my own father who would leave Mary and I without a sous."

"You are a fool. Any man who has learned the value of money would never permit a child of his to wed someone without any," the duke said.

William took a deep breath. "Of course, you would see it that way," he said quietly. "You have not once truly looked at Miss Durand. You have not seen the qualities she possesses – because they are not the qualities you are looking for. You could not care less if she is accomplished, kind, generous, clever, funny, or well-mannered. She does not have the money nor a vast estate for you to subsume into the Duchy, and so she will never be good enough."

"I should prefer you to wed someone who might offer all of those things – rather than simply the ones which have no possible value in the real world," his father said honestly.

"Like Miss Keyes? With her London townhouse, the manor house in Alnerton – and their newly built mansion in Norfolk?"

"And her father's carefully chosen investments that will make him money whether there is a good harvest or not from his lands," the duke said patiently as if explaining how the world worked to a small child. "And you did not seem to be averse to the match, just a few short months ago. You are fickle, my son. Your emotions are not a wise guide to what is best. How can you know how you will feel for Miss Durand even a month from now, when last quarter you seemed intent upon marrying another?"

William stared at his father, open-mouthed. Could he truly be so callous and unfeeling? William had always been sure that the duke had loved his mother. Her passing had certainly changed the duke, made him colder and more demanding. Yet he was now advocating his son live a half-life, wed to one who didn't love him and who he would never love.

"Father, do you not remember what it was like to be in love?" William asked sadly. "And do not tell me that love is not important. You loved Mama. I know you did."

The change in William's tone, or maybe his words seemed to shock the duke. He sank into a nearby chair and buried his head in his hands. "Yes, I loved your mother," he said, his voice almost a whisper, it was so choked with emotion. "And losing her broke my heart." He looked up at William. "I could not bear for you to have to go through that pain. I could not see that. It is better to live without love, then you cannot be hurt."

"I do not think that you believe that," William said. "You cannot wish me to be as miserable and unhappy as you have been since Mama passed away. And that is what you are asking of me, if you continue to try and force me away from Miss Durand. Losing her or losing you – either would be painful for me. Can you not see that?"

"You've already made your choice. So, go," the duke said wearily.

"And it would appear, that so have you. Farewell, Father."

William turned to leave, his heart breaking into tiny pieces. He loved his father. He always had, despite the duke's inability to show him love. He had not wanted things to come to this. Yet the old man's stubborn nature, his refusal to allow anything to happen any other way than his own, had brought them both to this parting.

"Wait," his father called out. William turned. "You would truly give everything up, for her?" he asked.

William nodded. "I would. I love her with all my heart. She, and her father, have taught me about the kind of man I want to be. One that can give and receive love without fear. One that takes chances but thinks through the possibilities before doing so. Someone who thinks for himself and looks at the world through different eyes – eyes that want to change things and make them better."

"Then I give you my blessing," the duke said simply, returning to his desk and sitting back down. He picked up his pen and began making entries in the ledger once more.

William stared at him. How could he be so calm after saying such a thing. "You mean it?" he asked, not daring to allow his joy to show.

"I do," the duke said, looking up from his books. "I want an heir. I want that heir to be you. You have finally proven to me that you will stand up for what you believe is right. You have just told me that you want to better, to do things differently." He paused, as if searching for the right words, to make William see why he had done what he had done.

"Can you not see that I have been breaking the mold for decades, here at Mormont?" William gave him a puzzled look. "You know well enough that I do not care one jot for a person's bloodlines."

"You don't?" William asked. He had certainly believed that was the main reason his father disapproved of Mary.

The duke laughed. "The men I chose for your sister, though they had good bloodlines, it was not their ancestors that I coveted for Charlotte. It was that they were men of business. They knew how to handle their own money, to manage their own estates – and to increase what they had been bequeathed."

"I still do not understand," William said.

"They were men of business. Too many of our class sit back and rely upon the wealth they have inherited. They expect it to magically keep increasing, so they might continue their lavish lifestyles."

"I have certainly seen my contemporaries fritter their allowances at card, and horses," William said thoughtfully. "They always overspend, having to ask their fathers for more."

"And that's just a tiny part of it, William. Houses like this cost vast amounts to run," the duke explained. "Their repair and upkeep require a king's ransom every single year. Estates and land can provide wealth – but only if managed well. The key to ensuring both is to take an interest and to make the decisions yourself – not leave them to unscrupulous managers and bailiffs. A new way is coming, and it will sweep away the old – because the old are too busy living the way they always have, assuming all will be as it has always been."

"But not Mormont," William said, the truth of his father's words sinking in.

"Exactly. It is why I have kept you at my side all these years. I hoped you would see what I was trying to do."

"Perhaps I have been a little blind, Father," William admitted.

"As perhaps was I. As you pointed out, not so very long ago, by not letting you make a few mistakes along the way, to test your knowledge, you could not learn the lessons I had hoped to teach you. I pray you will forgive me for being a bad teacher."

"I..." William tailed off, unsure if what he was hearing was real.

"Marry your girl. Perhaps she and her father will be the teachers you need," the duke said humbly. "As you say, they have come from nothing and made more of themselves than anyone might consider possible for those of their station. And give Mormont an heir who is a part of both the old world and the new."

❦

MARY SPENT AN ANXIOUS NIGHT. SHE WAS LOOKING forward to seeing her father, but the idea of leaving William filled her with dread. She knew it was for the best. And she also knew that she would somehow need to talk William out of his foolishness. He couldn't follow her. His place was here, at Caldor House. He was an earl and would one day be a duke. She would not be the one to make him give that up. And she could not bear to think that she might be the cause of a permanent rift between father and son, regardless of what William had said.

Papa arrived just before lunch. He bounced out of his

smart, new carriage and up the steps. Mary greeted him and accepted his joyful hug on the terrace outside the grand front doors. She was surprised to see the duke emerge from the house as she was about to explain to her father that they should perhaps eat at the inn in the village, before setting off for London.

The duke strode forward, his hand outstretched. "Good day to you, Mr. Durand. I am Frederick Pierce, the Duke of Mormont."

Papa looked confused. He didn't know whether to bow, as would normally be demanded at such a meeting, or to shake the man's hand. In the end, he tried to do both, and it was all rather ungainly. "Peter Durand, your Grace."

"Come inside, Cook has prepared a fine repast. I would be delighted if you would join us," the duke said, confounding Mary even more.

What was going on? Why was the duke being so kind to her father? He had spent months making her feel as though she was less valuable to him than the muck on his boots might be. She looked for William, hoping that he might be nearby, and might possibly be able to explain this unexpected change in behavior, but he was nowhere to be seen.

The duke escorted her father past the pile of trunks and vanity cases in the hallway, into the formal dining room. He offered Papa a seat at the foot of the table and took his usual seat at the head. Mary and Anne took their usual seats, silently, warily looking at the duke.

The uncomfortable silence was broken by the sound of carriage wheels and horses outside, and in moments Lady Charlotte, Captain James and little George, and William all took their seats at the table, too. Relieved to see some friendly faces and knowing that Charlotte would do what she could to make the meal less awkward, Mary tried to force a smile.

William beamed at her. She didn't know how he could be so cheerful. Lady Charlotte smiled at Mary and greeted Anne and Papa warmly, introducing her husband and son proudly. But rather than wearing her usual carefree smile, she kept looking from William to the duke, clearly as suspicious as Mary was that something wasn't quite right. Mary wished they had been in the drawing-room for this awkward greeting, at least that way she might have been able to speak with William or Charlotte to express her concerns and ask what was going on.

The soup was served, and the duke struck up a conversation with Papa about his trip to America. Mary watched him proudly detailing his business with his partner in Boston and the interest of the Duke of Compton. He talked at length of the meetings that he had attended whilst in America, and the ideas he had developed during his travels.

The duke listened attentively, genuinely interested. Mary was delighted that he was taking Papa seriously, but her sense of unease didn't leave her. She barely touched her soup, even though it was one of her favorites, cream of asparagus. A large beef and ale pie was served next, with fresh vegetables from the walled garden. Again, Mary could barely manage more than a mouthful or two.

Now, the duke was talking with William, about his intentions for the Duchy, and asking Papa his opinions on what might make good investments. Papa admitted it was something he was only beginning to learn about, from the Duke of Compton, but that he was flattered that the duke might think someone like him might offer the duke advice.

"I should be better placed, asking your Grace what I might do," Papa said with a warm smile.

"Advice I shall be glad to give," his Grace said generously.

"I must thank you for taking such care of Mary," her father said looking around the table. "I was so worried about leaving her alone in London. And now I know that she was unwell, too – well, I am glad she was amongst people who so clearly care for her very much."

Lady Charlotte and William both smiled. Captain Watts looked uncomfortable at the compliment but flushed slightly, and so Mary knew he was pleased by it. The duke, however, had the decency to look a little guilty. "I must confess," he admitted, "I was not always inclined towards Miss Durand. I owe her, and Miss Knorr, my most profound apologies for my behavior. I was quick to judge and too stubborn to see what was right in front of my eyes – and for that, I am truly sorry."

"You are most gladly forgiven," Mary said warmly. Anne nodded her agreement. She rarely found her voice when the duke was present. He scared her with his quick-silver moods and disapproving glares.

The servants cleared the plates away and brought in individual desserts, each one covered with a silver dome. "You should try yours, first," William said, grinning. "I asked Cook to prepare your favorite."

Cautiously, Mary lifted the dome from her plate. With all eyes upon her, she had never felt more conspicuous. As she lifted the dome away, to reveal a perfectly decorated plate, with a *gimblette de fleurs d'orange* and a carefully crafted sugar paste swan. Nestled within its partly furled wings, on its downy back, lay a diamond ring. Mary gasped.

William stood up and moved to kneel before her. "Miss Mary Durand, will you do me the honor of being my wife?" he asked her, to squeals of delight from Lady Charlotte and a whoop from Captain Watts.

Mary glanced around the table, from her father, to Anne, to Charlotte, James, George, and then back to William. "But..." she started, then looked at the duke.

"That ring is the one I gave William's mother when I asked for her hand," he informed her and smiled warmly.

"He gave you his blessing," she whispered to William, who nodded.

"He did, as did your Father, who I met on the road on his way here to ask for his permission to ask for your hand."

"You rode out to ask Papa," she said, tears of joy threatening to pour down her cheeks.

"Yes, so given that everyone else around this table is fully in favor of us making a match, could you please let me know if you are, too?"

"Oh, William," Mary sighed, happier than she could ever remember being. "How could you even think there could be any other answer than, yes. I should be delighted to be your wife."

William raised her to her feet, and embraced her, pressing a chaste kiss to her forehead – though the innocent caress of his lips sent a frisson of sensations flooding through her entire body. In moments, she had been embraced, or kissed, or congratulated by everyone present. Lady Charlotte had tears in her eyes, as did Anne and Papa looked so proud as he held her tightly. Mary had never been so happy. She kept looking at the duke, expecting him to rant and rail and put a stop to everything, but he was the one to slip the ring upon her finger. "My beloved wife would have championed you from the start," he admitted quietly. "I cannot tell you how happy it makes me to see her ring upon your finger. Look after my boy. I know you will love him – but ensure he does not do anything too reckless."

"I promise. I shall care for him until my dying day," Mary assured him. "And I will do my best to make you proud."

William caught her around the waist and pulled her away. "Must we have a long engagement," he asked her, causing everyone to pull faces as if they were shocked.

"No, as soon as the banns are read will do," she said with a grin.

EPILOGUE

The bells of the village church rang out, reaching even as far as Caldor House. William stepped out onto the terrace and looked out over the grounds of the house. The usually immaculate lawns were filled with all manner of stalls and amusements. Father had decided that he wanted there to be a fair, that all his tenants could attend and enjoy, to celebrate the wedding of his son to Miss Mary Durand.

Inside, there was to be a fine wedding breakfast in the formal dining room for fifty people, and a ball for the local gentry. William didn't care how his father chose to celebrate it he was just glad that he did want to celebrate. He had come so close to losing his home, and his family – and he would still give them up for Mary, because she was his world.

The sound of a carriage coming up the driveway made William turn. James perched on the box of William's phaeton, driving the pair of horses with skill. He brought the carriage to a stop. William put on his top hat, smoothed down his jacket and fiddled with his silk cravat, then bounded down the steps to greet his friend. "Are you ready?" James asked him.

"I am," William said. "I think I've been waiting for this day for a very long time."

James whipped the horses to a canter, the sporty coach tearing along the lanes and into the village. William slapped his friend on the back. "Would you like to borrow this for a little longer?" he asked.

"I wouldn't say no, but I think your sister might object. George would want to learn to drive it – and she would never forgive me if there was an accident, and he was on board."

"Come over whenever you wish to blow out a few cobwebs, my old friend," William said. "I'll not tell her or George."

They made their way inside the church. The entire village had turned out, and people were spilling out of the back of the nave, the local gentry having taken up the seats to the front by the altar. William greeted a few he knew, shaking hands and asking after their health. He was delighted to see a number of the cottagers had come, too. Mary had made such an impact on so many people locally, even though she'd been here such a short time.

His father had sent men from the village, carpenters and skilled workmen, to go and fix up the houses on the outskirts of Alnerton. They'd dug a new well, and the duke had offered every man there a permanent place on the estate. Some had refused, but his father had not turned anyone out. He'd brought their rents into line and had taken over their collection, making them part of the regular quarter day, like everyone else. William was delighted to see how many of them doffed their cap as his Father arrived and took his seat in the front pew.

The newly acquired church organ played merry tunes as everyone took their seats and settled. Then there was a brief moment of silence, before the reverend appeared at the end of the aisle, followed by four altar boys, one carrying a large gold cross, the others clasping their hands in prayer. The small party made their way down the aisle, each taking their place before the organ began to play the wedding march.

William took a deep breath and turned to see Mary walking slowly towards him, her arm tucked through her father's, her face glowing with happiness. She wore an ivory silk gown, with tiny seed pearls embroidered into the bodice, and her glorious blonde curls were full of tiny white flowers and more seed pearls that glinted in the light. Each time she stepped forward he saw that she was wearing matching satin slippers. She looked perfectly radiant.

He smiled at her and held her gaze until she stood beside him and Mr. Durand placed her hand in William's. "God bless you, my son, my daughter," he said, his voice choked with emotion, then kissed Mary's cheek and stepped back.

Bride and groom stared into one another's eyes. The vicar welcomed the congregation, but they barely heard a word of it, they were so lost in one another. Somehow, they managed to repeat their vows when prompted and William slipped a simple gold band onto Mary's finger when told to do so. He accepted the kiss of peace from the vicar and passed it to Mary.

And then they were married. They walked back down the aisle, hand in hand, walking on air, enjoying the smiles and happiness of everyone present. William could hardly believe his luck. He was married to the woman he loved.

His father had given his blessing, and more importantly, Mary loved him as he loved her. He thought there was nothing more on earth that could make him happier than he was right now.

When they arrived back at Caldor House, the fair had already begun. People milled around, drinking, laughing, dancing, and enjoying the amusements. William and Mary walked through the festivities, greeting everyone and taking part in a lively jig with some of the villagers before they made their way up to the house, where some of their closest friends were waiting for them.

William delighted in introducing Mary to everyone she hadn't already met, and she introduced him to some of the people she had met in London, through his friends, before they all sat down to the lavish wedding breakfast that Cook had slaved over for days.

With everyone full and content, William led Mary into the ballroom, where a string quartet was playing a waltz. "I love you Lady Mary Pierce, Countess Cott," William whispered as they danced cheek to cheek. Mary gasped and stared at him. She had not thought once about the fact that she would now share his title.

"Oh, that sounds so strange," she said, her beautiful blue eyes wide.

"And, one day you shall be a duchess," he reminded her, as James and Charlotte joined them on the dance floor, followed by Charlotte's old companion, Sophie Lefebvre and the man who had unwittingly brought William and Mary together once more, Claveston St. John.

"I shall do my best not to let you down," Mary said, a little nervously.

"Darling Mary, don't you know you could never do that," William said, pouring all his love into his words.

"You are perfect, in every way. You have taught me so much, and I promise to love you forever. I will do all that is in my power to do, to make you happy."

"Just be happy yourself," Mary told him. "If you are happy, then I will be happy. I love you, William. I always have and I always will."

William sighed and pulled her closer. "I cannot tell you how happy I am to know that."

AH, TOGETHER AGAIN! I HOPE YOU ENJOYED WILLIAM and Mary's happy ever after story. Did you miss the first book in this series? Please check out Loving the Scarred Soldier

MY DEAR READER

Thank you for reading and supporting my books! I hope this story brought you some escape from the real world into the always captivating Regency world. A good story, especially one with a happy ending, just brightens your day and makes you feel good! If you enjoyed the book, would you leave a review on Amazon? Reviews are always appreciated.

Below is a complete list of all my books! Why not click and see if one of them can keep you entertained for a few hours?

The Returned Lords of Grosvenor Square
The Returned Lords of Grosvenor Square: A Regency
Romance Boxset
The Waiting Bride
The Long Return
The Duke's Saving Grace
A New Home for the Duke

The Spinsters Guild
A New Beginning
The Disgraced Bride
A Gentleman's Revenge
A Foolish Wager
A Lord Undone

Convenient Arrangements
A Broken Betrothal
In Search of Love
Wed in Disgrace
Betrayal and Lies
A Past to Forget
Engaged to a Friend

Landon House
Mistaken for a Rake
A Selfish Heart
A Love Unbroken
A Christmas Match
A Most Suitable Bride
An Expectation of Love

Second Chance Regency Romance
Loving the Scarred Soldier

Second Chance for Love

Christmas Stories
Love and Christmas Wishes: Three Regency Romance
Novellas
A Family for Christmas
Mistletoe Magic: A Regency Romance
Home for Christmas Series Page

Happy Reading!
All my love,
Rose

A SNEAK PEAK OF LOVING THE SCARRED SOLDIER

PROLOGUE

C *aldor House, Alnerton, 1807*

"I WILL GET YOU, LADY CHARLOTTE PIERCE," JAMES whispered into her ear as he leaned just a smidge closer.

Charlotte looked over her shoulder to where Mrs. Crosby, her plump companion, was walking some feet behind them.

"Oh no you will not, James Watts, for I already have you," Charlotte replied cheekily, a playful grin on her face which exaggerated her dimples and the small cleft in her chin.

"Ah, but you only think that you have me. Truth be told, I have already laid claim to you these many years, but I allowed you to believe otherwise." He raised his chin slightly, the sun shining down on his handsome face. "There is no escaping it."

James folded his arms behind his back and Charlotte

peered up at him. James and her brother William were the same age, but James was minutely taller, with broader shoulders and a more relaxed air about him. William, unfortunately, was often far too austere – a characteristic for which he could thank their father, the Duke of Mormont.

Charlotte kept watching James in silence, waiting until he turned back in her direction. The moment he did, she grinned at him and promptly stuck out her tongue.

"You always like to best me James, but I tell you, one day, I will be the one who claims victory. Not you."

He grinned, his bright smile illuminating his oval face and gently sloping cheekbones.

"I look forward to it. You could win me over for the rest of my life," he whispered.

Charlotte's heart fluttered in her chest.

"You should not say such things, James," she replied. "Someone might think you mean what you say."

Her fingers rose to coil a tress of dark brown hair. She wrapped it around her index finger several times as she kept her eyes to the ground, waiting for his reply.

"You know I always mean what I say," he answered tersely.

Charlotte's feet faltered with her heart. What was he saying? Lately, James's conversations were more and more personal, much more than they ever had been before. They'd long had a closeness between them, ever since her former governess, Mrs. Northam, had married his father, John, who acted as the Duchy of Mormont's solicitor. Now, however, things were changing.

Slowly, she looked up at him again and was met by the intensity of his emerald eyes. It made her heart gallop. She could not maintain the connection and quickly looked away.

"James, do not toy with me."

"I would never toy with you about such things," he replied calmly.

Again, Charlotte's eyes could not refrain from looking at him. In recent years she had often found herself admiring the man he had become. He was no longer the boy she'd run after and played games with all those years ago. He was a man of twenty, two years her elder, and more esteemed in her sight than any of their acquaintances, save her brother.

Charlotte stopped walking when she realized that James had failed to follow. She turned to face him, perplexity filling her heart. These feelings were strange to her. She had no mother to teach her, and with Mrs. Northam, now Mrs. Watts, no longer in her family employ, she was left to decipher the world on her own, for her nurse, Mrs. Crosby, was not someone whom she felt she could ask about important matters.

"Charlotte."

The sound of her name on his lips was a cherished utterance. She was very fond of it, more than she ever dared to admit. They knew each other too well - what she felt could not be what she thought it was. Could it? When he looked at her the way he was doing now, she believed that it could be.

"We have known each other for what seems a lifetime," James continued. The soft timbre of his voice was soothing. "We have played together and argued, cried, and laughed. We have seen each other in every... circumstance."

She laughed as the memory of their foray into his family's lakes, in nothing more than their undergarments as children suddenly flashed into her mind. Her father had been most upset by the indiscreet incident, which had left her soaked through, on the eve of a special dinner party. He had been equally displeased with the subsequent chill that had confined her to her bed. None of which had bothered her.

"We have."

James' brow furrowed slightly and she had the urge to smooth the wrinkles with her thumb. Customarily, she would have done so, but at that moment, with her feelings teetering on the brink, she dared not, lest they both fall over the edge.

Charlotte watched in curious fascination as the lump in James' throat bobbed up and down, and her dashing friend, ever confident, seemed to falter in his words. It was surprisingly endearing to see him so undone. She bit back a smile, but still felt the tug of it on her cheeks.

"You have to know... that is... you must be aware," James stuttered. His eyes were still lowered to his feet, but then, in a sudden burst of confidence, he forced himself to meet her gaze.

"Aware of what?" Charlotte questioned.

It took all of her strength to muster the words of the questions which curiosity demanded be answered. Did he feel as she did? Did his heart flutter at the sight of her as hers did whenever she saw him? Did he get cold, and his skin prickle when they touched? Was his head as full of her as hers was of him?

The more she thought of it, the more her emotions threatened to get the better of her. She quickly turned away, sure that her feelings were now evident on her face. She did not want to lose to him in this. She did not want to be the first to make her feelings known. In this one thing, she wanted to best him.

Charlotte's heart thundered in her ears. Her hands folded into defiant fists, as she determined not to be swayed by her emotions. She would be strong. She would let him speak and not give herself away, though she was aware that she may have already done so.

"Charlotte?" James' voice was a whisper. Then, she felt his hands settle gently on her arms. She was acutely aware of the proximity of his body to hers. This was not their normal interaction. Yes, they were close, had even embraced, but the feelings which filled her at that moment were far greater, more powerful – consuming. Her stomach felt as if it would take flight. "You feel it too, don't you?" he continued to whisper.

"Feel what?" Charlotte replied as her voice shook.

She glanced in the direction of Mrs. Crosby. The woman was pretending to look at the leaves on one of the potted plants, but glances in their direction made Charlotte aware that she was keeping a close eye on them, in case things went too far.

"She will not come. I asked her not to."

Charlotte's eyes widened and her breath caught in her throat at James' confession.

"You did what?"

"I asked Mrs. Crosby to give us a moment of privacy," he continued. "There is something very particular which I wish to say to you, Charlotte. Something best said to your face and not your back."

She could hear the slight lilt of laughter in his voice, but also nervousness.

"James," she replied. "You can tell me anything. You always have."

Her words were answered with a gentle tug on her arms, turning her to face him. She did not resist. She could not. All strength was gone from her limbs and she was at the mercy of her feelings, which would not be hidden.

Their eyes met and Charlotte thought she might faint. Her head felt light, her heart was gone, only large butterfly wings remained, beating frantically in her chest, as smaller ones filled her belly. What was happening?

He did not remove his hands from her arms, Instead, he stepped closer, and Charlotte felt sure that the world had stopped and she no longer remembered how to breathe.

"You and William have always been my dearest friends," James stated. "But you, Charlotte, you have become something infinitely more dear to me." Warmth washed up her neck and she was sure that her cheeks were now painted in crimson. Yet she could not speak. "I know that you have only ever considered me as a friend, and for a long time, I had accepted that fact. I thought I could live with it, but I cannot. I cannot be content with simply being your friend when I desire to be something much more."

Charlotte raised a hand and placed it on his chest to stop him, but the beating beneath her fingers caused her to pause. His heart was racing just like hers.

James looked at her delicate fingers and then placed his hand over hers, holding it over his heart.

"This is what I feel every time I am near you. I cannot stop it. I have tried, but nothing works. I think it is because I do not wish it to. I like that you do this to me. You are the only one who can."

Her breathing erratic, Charlotte tried to think. She knew all the proper things to do, the decorum that was required, but how did one have such decorum with someone who had nursed your wounds and wiped your tears, often after having been responsible for causing them? One who knew you better than anyone else did?

"I know there are many who desire you," James continued. "I am not so foolish as to believe that I am the only one who cares for you, but I would hope I might have some advantage over those others."

"Of whom do you speak? I know of no one," Charlotte questioned, bewildered.

His emerald eyes were ablaze.

"Do you mean to tell me that there is no other who wishes your hand?"

Charlotte's hearing became hollow, only the sound of what seemed to be rushing water could be heard as the words left his lips. She was eighteen. She had never had anyone desire her hand, at least not that she knew of. Such matters were for her father, and none dared speak to her before presenting their proposal to him. None but James, that is. He was allowed certain liberties that other gentlemen were not, being such a close family friend.

"What are you saying?" she whispered, "Be plain."

He smiled at her.

"Always so straightforward."

"Always skirting around the subject," she replied. "Just tell me. Do not keep me on tenterhooks." She squeezed his hand lightly. "I want to hear the words."

James stepped closer, the space between them almost entirely gone as he lowered his head to her ear and whispered.

"I love you, Charlotte. I have always loved you."

The smile his words elicited could not be contained, and as their eyes met, she answered him.

"I love you, too, James. I always have."

CALDOR HOUSE, ALNERTON, 1809

"LADY CHARLOTTE. LADY CHARLOTTE." A SOFT VOICE repeated her name, but Charlotte was doing her utmost to resist. "You must rouse yourself, Lady Charlotte. The day is already upon us and you must get ready."

It was Sophie Lefebvre, her new companion. Her father had finally been swayed to Charlotte's view that Mrs. Crosby was no longer suitable and that a woman closer to her age would be a far better choice. Sophie, who was also almost twenty, the daughter of an Englishwoman and a Frenchman, her family in exile from France as a result of the war, had seemed a good choice to replace Mrs. Crosby.

Charlotte forced her dark brown eyes open. The room was still mostly in darkness, but Sophie had the chamber-maids already at work opening the blinds, while she set about laying out Charlotte's attire in readiness.

"Please, Lady Charlotte. You do not want to keep your brother and the duke waiting. It would be disrespectful to Monsieur Watts if you were to arrive late," Sophie pleaded. "You would not want to do that."

Sophie knew those words would force Charlotte from her bed, though no words could change how Charlotte felt, not on that day.

Charlotte forced herself to rise from her four-poster bed, then padded to the window, her bare feet making no noise as she crossed the room. She looked out to where grey mists covered the gardens. The sky was overcast and the sun was completely hidden. It was as if the day shared her feelings.

"Quickly, Lady Charlotte," Sophie continued. She came to stand beside Charlotte. "I know that you do not wish to go, but you must."

"Must I?" Charlotte retorted weakly. "It will change nothing."

Sophie sighed.

"No, it will not. It is not supposed to. It is for you to show the respect which Monsieur Watts deserves. Please, come from the window and let me help you dress."

Charlotte was a doll in Sophie's hands. She turned her and twisted her, made her sit, and stand, all while Charlotte uttered not a word. Finally, once her shoes were on and her black dress laced and every adornment in place, she sat her before the mirror.

The young woman who looked back at her was foreign to her eyes. Her skin was far paler than it used to be. Her eyes less bright and her long dark brown hair seemed a dull greyish-black. Everything seemed to be cast in shades of grey.

The white collar which rose around her neck itched, but Charlotte cared little about it. It was the only contrast to the black of the rest of her ensemble. Once her hair was curled and pinned, Sophie placed a black feathered cap on her head.

"C'est fini! You are done!"

Charlotte didn't reply. Instead, she stood and strode out of her chamber.

She found William loitering in the hall, waiting for her. Her brother was not himself either, as was evident from the solemn expression on his face. He walked toward her and took her hand, hooking it gently over his arm.

"How are you this morning, Charlotte? We missed you at breakfast."

"How should I be?" she answered absently.

Her eyes glanced over the balcony to the floor below.

"It was a foolish question," William replied. "Forgive me. I do not know how to deal with these matters."

She turned to her brother.

"Save Mother, we are unaccustomed to such things. You are forgiven."

He smiled at her before proceeding, in silence, to escort her down the stairs and out the door, to where the carriage waited for them. It was decorated appropriately; pulled by matched black horses with black plumes upon their heads. The driver was similarly dressed in black and the carriage was of the same color.

Charlotte's feet faltered, but William bore her up and helped her inside. Their father was already waiting.

"That took you too long," he commented harshly. "It isn't right to be late for such things. It is gross disrespect, Charlotte. You should know better. Both of you."

"Forgive me, Father," William replied. "It was my fault entirely."

"All the worse. You, being the elder, should direct your sister appropriately, and not pander to such poor conduct. See to it that it never happens again."

"Of course, Father. Never again," William replied.

Charlotte remained silent, and as the carriage moved forward, her gaze stayed fixed out the window.

She recognized none of the landscape as they passed, her mind too full to allow her to truly see what was before her, and she shunned the sight of Watton Hall, James' former home. She could not look upon it without losing her composure. She chose to close her eyes until she was sure they were well past it. The next sight she saw, consequently, was that of Alnerton Village Church.

The chapel was overflowing with mourners, but a special place had been reserved for them, and William helped her to it. Charlotte sat in silence, refusing to look at the empty coffin at the front of the church.

James was not there. His body had been lost somewhere in Roliça, Portugal, where he'd fallen during the battle with the French the year before. It had taken months for them to get news of his death, and more still for his father to come to terms with it, enough to have the memorial service held.

They all struggled to believe it – Captain James Watts, a fine young man, his father's pride and joy, an adoring stepson and caring and devoted friend, and the man Charlotte loved, was dead.

The Reverend Moore said a great many things about James, but they were only shadows of the truth. James was far more than the vicar claimed. The vicar hadn't known James as she did.

She could have told them of the man he truly was, the gentle soul who'd tended her knee when she fell among the brambles. The man who'd taken every opportunity to touch her hand whenever he could, and who had loved to make her laugh.

The man whose face she still saw every time she closed her eyes.

Once the rites were performed, Charlotte and her family gathered with Mr and Mrs Watts to bury the son they'd lost.

She was coping, in control, until the moment the pallbearers brought the coffin to the grave. Then, Charlotte lost all semblance of calm.

The tears flowed from her eyes and her body was wracked with uncontrollable spasms. She gasped for breath but found none. She was suffocating where she stood. The air she struggled to breathe was gone. James was gone.

William did his best to console her, but there was no consolation for her grief - it was a physical pain she could not bear, and she crumbled under the weight of it. Seconds later, her brother's strong arms were carrying her away from the sight, away from sympathetic, pitying eyes, to the safety of their carriage. Their father followed close behind, and soon they were on their way home.

Charlotte had no recollection of the return journey. Her room was dark when she awoke, much later, and she was still dressed in her mourning gown. Her feathered cap was gone.

She rolled onto her back but no sooner had she done so than fresh tears rolled down her cheeks. He was gone. James was never coming back.

It was heartbreak like no other. She had been a child, barely two, when her mother had passed away, and she had no true recollection of that loss. James, though, was different. She had known him. She had cared for him. She had loved him.

Silent tears kept her company as she lay in the dark until her eyes could weep no more. Then, Charlotte forced herself to sit up. The gloom of her room was oppressive - she needed to escape it, she needed light to help her fight the darkness which threatened to overtake her. She rushed to her chamber door, forgetting to don stockings or shoes, and simply walked along the corridor with no plan of where she was going.

Soon, she heard her father's voice. She followed it until she stood outside his office. She listened; he was in conversation with someone - her brother William she was sure - and she heard her name mentioned.

"The Marquess of Dornthorpe?" her brother asked.

"Yes. He has written to propose his interest in an alliance between our families. He is seeking your sister's hand for his son, Malcolm, Earl of Benton."

"Father, it is too soon to present such a proposal to Charlotte. She is still mourning for James."

"She will recover. Such an alliance should be most agreeable to all parties. However, I note your point. I will give her a few weeks to mourn his loss before informing her of the betrothal."

"Betrothal? Father, don't you think it prudent to ask Charlotte if she has any interest in the man before arranging an engagement. She has met him but four times, if I remember right. And a betrothal during mourning — that will set the gossips' tongues wagging."

"Four times was more than enough for your mother to decide to marry me. I do not see why your sister should be any different. As for the gossips — well, technically, James is no relation of ours, and so mourning is not a requirement."

"Father, please..."

"I have made my decision, William. Your sister will marry Malcolm Tate, and become the Countess of Benton, and eventually the Marchioness of Dornthorpe. Our family will sit on two seats, Dornthorpe and Mormont. Such a fortunate alliance is to be envied indeed."

Her knees gave out and the floor rushed up, as Charlotte slumped against the wall. That was it? James was barely in his grave and yet she was given to another? It was at that moment that she realized how conniving her father truly was. He cared nothing for her pain and hurt, only for their family's good standing.

Charlotte had no strength to remove herself from outside the door. *Let them find me here*, she thought. *Let them know that I am aware of what they had discussed without her. Let them see what it has done to me. Maybe that would touch father's heart.*

She might hope so, but she suspected it was unlikely.

CHAPTER 1

aldor House, Alnerton, 1814

CHARLOTTE LOOKED UP AT THE IMPOSING BUILDING toward which they were driving. Caldor House was still the same, all these years later, and as it had in the past, it filled her heart with heaviness. The only reason she was returning to her father's home was for the sake of her son. George needed a male influence, and without his father, he had only her father and William to guide him, for her late husband's father now had suffered a debilitating illness.

She looked over to where her sleeping child lay. He was so much like Malcolm that it made her smile to think of it. She stroked his hair gently. She had not loved Malcolm when she'd married him, but he was the escape she'd needed – from grief and from loneliness.

In return, she had given him the gift of their son – the

son he had hoped for, to carry on his family name. She was happy that she'd been able to do so before his time on earth was over. Her only regret was that he would not be there to see George grow into a man he would be proud of.

The carriage stopped on the broad expanse of gravel in front of the house. The door opened, and there, standing in his usual fine attire, was her brother William. A broad smile spread across his face as he immediately took the stairs at a rapid pace to come toward her.

"Charlotte!" he called.

She smiled in return as the coachman opened the door for her and helped her down.

"William, how wonderful to see you."

She wrapped her arms around him. It felt like a lifetime since they had last seen each other, and she had missed him dearly - it was his presence here, more than anything, which had brought her back to her childhood home.

"How was your journey?" William asked.

"Long and tiring. George is asleep in the carriage," Charlotte replied.

"Then I shall gather him up and carry him into the house."

William strode toward the carriage and, moments later, cradled her son in his arms. George looked angelic, nestled against his uncle's chest, completely safe from all harm.

It wasn't easy being alone and so far from home. Once Malcolm had died, everything had changed. Suddenly the security Charlotte knew no longer existed. There was also the threat from those who wished to take from her son what was rightfully his, the title of Earl of Benton, and, likely quite soon, that of Marquess of Dornthorpe, when his ailing grandfather died. He was too young, but he would learn under her father, and when he was old enough, he would return and take his place. In the meantime, Malcolm's trusted steward, Mr. Charlesworth, was tending to matters and would send Charlotte regular reports.

"He weighs nothing," William commented as they walked up the stairs.

"To you perhaps, but to me, he weighs little less than a ton," Charlotte mused. "Is Father at home?"

William's expression fell.

"He had to remain in town to see to some pressing matters with our bankers. I have only just returned myself. I wanted to be here for your arrival. Father will return by tea time."

Charlotte nodded in understanding - it was for the best that her father was not present. It gave her time to settle herself, to some extent, before seeing him again. Since her marriage, Charlotte had seen little of her father. He had stayed in Alnerton or at their townhouse in London and found no reason to visit her, not even at the birth of his grandson, although he had sent a card and an expensive gift.

"I have prepared your old rooms for you and converted the adjoining suite into a nursery for George. I thought it best to keep him near you. He will be unfamiliar with these surroundings for a time."

Charlotte smiled.

"Thank you, William. You think of everything."

"I try to," he replied with a grin. "Especially when it comes to matters of my sister and nephew."

They were greeted at the door by almost all of the household staff, their smiling faces bright as they welcomed her back. Charlotte was slightly overwhelmed.

She'd almost forgotten them, for she had put Caldor House behind her on the day she'd left, thinking she would never return to it. Unfortunately, fate had other plans for her, and here she was.

Once the welcome was over, she followed William upstairs as footmen scurried to unload all of her possessions and carry the steamer trunks up to her rooms. William carried George into the nursery and settled him into bed without him even waking. Leaving a nursemaid watching over him as he slept, William opened the door and ushered her through into her rooms.

The space was bright, the curtains pulled wide to allow the sun into the room, but the memories lingered there. She could remember the last night she'd spent in that room, and the many before that, filled with hopes, fears, and then abiding grief.

I thought never to see this room again, yet, here I am.

"Is everything to your liking?" William said from behind her.

Charlotte turned to him, slowly untying the ribbon from beneath her chin as she removed her bonnet.

"Everything is just as I remember it."

"I wanted it to be as easy an adjustment for you as possible."

He smiled at her.

"I missed you very much," Charlotte replied.

Sadness began to prick her eyes with tears.

"And I, you," William replied as she strode toward him.

She fell into her brother's embrace and held him tightly as memories overwhelmed her. His hand gently patted her back as he spoke soothingly in her ear.

"I know it has been frightfully difficult for you, Charlotte. I wish I could have made it better. A thousand times

I have wished I could have changed the things that happened, but I hope you know I had no control over those circumstances."

"Hush," Charlotte urged. "Do not speak of it. I know what you would have done if you could." She looked up at him. "Now, leave me alone for a while. I shall rest before tea."

"Of course."

William nodded and excused himself.

She lay back on the bed intending to rest, but her mind resisted that intent. Memories tumbled through her mind, leaving her wide awake and out of sorts. She lay on her bed, her hands clasped over her stomach as she looked up at the canopy above her, until the exhaustion from the long day of travel, and all that had gone before, caught up with her, and sleep overtook her.

It was nearly teatime when Charlotte awoke. Immediately, she worried about George, but when she called for the maid, she was assured that George had eaten his meal, had looked in to see his mother sleeping, and had happily gone back into the nursery with the maid, to play with his toys.

Charlotte allowed the maid to dress her in a gown suitable for dining with her father. Her father kept an elegant table at all times and expected everyone to conform to his expectations.

Her dress was mint green in color, made from the finest silk and lace. It had been a gift from Malcolm before he became ill. Charlotte was glad that, now her mourning was done, she could wear colors again. The year of mourning had taken a toll on her, shut away at Bentonmere Park, but it had also been peaceful. Now, for George's sake, it was time to be visible to the world again.

She smoothed her hands over her stomach as she looked at her reflection in the mirror. Her shape had changed after having George. She no longer had a girl's figure, but it was a pleasing figure nonetheless. She twisted a curl of dark hair around her finger then pushed it back into place before turning away.

The dining room was set when Charlotte arrived. William lingered by the door waiting for her.

"Father isn't here as yet," he informed her.

"Shall we sit then and wait?"

"We may as well. You know how he is about punctuality, even if he is not so himself," her brother answered with a light laugh.

He hooked his arm and held it out to her.

Charlotte allowed her brother his little trifles of amusement. He'd had so little of humor in his youth, for he'd lived under their father's thumb, ever aware that he was to inherit his title and position, as Duke, and also his vast portfolio of investments, in banking and shipping. It had always been a heavy burden for William to bear, and because of that, Charlotte hardly ever allowed herself the luxury of sharing her burdens with her brother.

James had always been the person she'd shared such things with.

The thought of her former love gave her a moment of pause. It always did. Despite his death, James Watts had really never left her, even throughout her marriage, he was, in a way, ever-present. He was still a comfort to her in her thoughts, even if he was no longer in the world.

"How are Father's affairs?" she questioned once they were seated.

William sighed.

"When it comes to matters pertaining to the smooth

running of the Duchy, it is never a straightforward task. Father insists upon seeing to every detail, no matter how small. He leaves me little responsibility – though he expects me to pay as close attention as he does himself."

She looked at him with concern. He was clearly frustrated at the lack of trust their father was showing him.

"Do you like it at all? Working with Father, I mean?"

"There are days when I love it. Learning about all the elements involved in the Duchy's management, from managing the rents to investing the proceeds from the land well – it is absorbing and challenging. Many in Father's place would entrust such work to managers and bailiffs – but he prides himself that it is a matter of honor."

"Has there been some cause for a loss?"

Charlotte shook her head lightly. Her brother was a clever man. He had left Cambridge with high praise from his tutors, and he was not one to shirk his duties. But Father was very demanding. It could only be hard on William to have to always listen and never be permitted to give his opinion or have any autonomy.

They were sipping wine and talking when their father finally arrived. He marched into the room without care or apology and promptly seated himself at the head of the table.

"Charlotte," he stated. "I am glad to see that you that have arrived and remembered how I prefer to go on here."

"Thank you, Father."

"Where is the boy?"

"George is with Mrs. White, his nurse. He will be in bed by now."

"Good, a boy needs routine and order - structure makes a man," her father continued. He picked up the small bell which sat to his right and rang it, as an indication to the staff to serve dinner.

The meal was delicious - four courses as usual - including dessert. Her father always insisted upon it, although why she never knew. It was simply the way it was.

"How is Mrs. Watts, William? Has she improved at all?" her father asked through a mouthful of the roast.

"I'm afraid not, Father. Mr Watts told me only yesterday that she has taken a turn for the worse."

"Unfortunate. We are sure to have a funeral to attend soon," her father continued.

Charlotte dropped her knife in alarm.

"Funeral? Is Mrs. Watts so ill?"

"I am afraid so," William explained. "It has been several months now since she first became ill and there seems to be no end in sight. I am sorry to have to tell you this on your first day back."

She could hardly think. Beatrice Watts was the only mother figure Charlotte had ever known. The thought of her death was unbearable. How would her husband take that news after already having lost James?

"I will go to see her tomorrow," Charlotte blurted.

It was her father's turn to drop his cutlery. However, he recovered quickly and carried on as if nothing had happened.

"I do not think that is wise, Charlotte. Mrs. Watts is very ill and you have a child to consider. You cannot allow yourself to be so exposed."

"What exposure can there be, Father? I will take the customary precautions. I am sure that you and William have visited her, and neither of you has become ill."

"I think Father is correct, Charlotte. You have only just

returned here, perhaps you should allow yourself some time to adjust before visiting the Watts," William agreed.

She looked at him perplexed.

"William, Mrs. Watts has tended to us our entire lives. How can I be so unfair as to avoid her, especially under these circumstances? I cannot. I will not. I shall visit her tomorrow."

The subject died immediately, but Charlotte did not miss the silent exchange between her brother and father, an exchange of looks which puzzled her completely. She did not understand their thinking but she would not be persuaded by it. Mrs. Watts was a lovely woman and she would see her, and care for her if it would give her any comfort at all.

After tea, Charlotte retreated to the parlor, but she was not alone for long. Mrs. White brought George to her soon after, the young child having woken fretful and calling for her. She set her son on the floor with his blocks and joined him.

"A little of this and you will be tired again in no time, won't you George?" she said as she placed one block on top of the other. George hit the floor with his.

They continued like that for several minutes before they were joined by William. Her brother watched them with a silent grin as they played. His presence was comforting and Charlotte was happy to have him there and thankful that their father was absent.

"I am sorry I could not stay long after the funeral," William said suddenly.

Charlotte looked at him perplexed.

"Why do you bring it up?"

"I do not think I have apologized enough for it. You

needed me after his passing and I could not be there for you as I should."

"William, you had pressing work. I understood," Charlotte assured him.

William had only stayed a fortnight after Malcolm was laid to rest. Charlotte had wanted him to stay longer, but the management of the estates and the investments had called him away, and she could not bring herself to ask him to prolong his stay regardless. She held no grudge toward him for it. It was the way of the world, and her loss was no large factor in his life, only hers.

"Thank you, Charlotte. You have always been too kind in everything," William continued. "Do you still intend to visit Mrs. Watts tomorrow?"

"Of course," she replied. "I said I would and I shall do so. I shall make arrangements in the morning to visit her during the afternoon."

William was silent for a moment. Charlotte could see he was contemplating something, more than likely the bank, or next year's crop plantings on one of the estates – he never stopped thinking of such things, it seemed to her.

"Will you excuse me, Charlotte? I have a matter I must urgently attend to."

"Of course."

William came to them and ruffled George's hair before leaving the room. Charlotte remained with her son, playing with his blocks until his eyes grew heavy again, and he curled beside her on the floor to sleep.

She lifted George and carried him from the room, leaving the blocks where they lay, holding his head gently against her shoulder as she walked toward the stairs and their rooms. On her way up, she happened to turn, and glance down, to see William giving a letter to a footman, who immediately left the house. Her brow furrowed. Who was William writing to at such an hour?

THERE IS A HUGE SECRET THAT LADY CHARLOTTE discovers and it will change her life! Check out the rest of the story in the Kindle Store Loving the Scarred Soldier

JOIN MY MAILING LIST

Sign up for my newsletter to stay up to date on new releases, contests, giveaways, freebies, and deals!

Free book with signup!

Monthly Facebook Giveaways! Books and Amazon gift cards! Join me on Facebook: https://www. facebook.com/rosepearsonauthor

Website: www.RosePearsonAuthor.com

Follow me on Goodreads: Author Page

You can also follow me on Bookbub! Click on the picture below – see the Follow button?

JOIN MY MAILING LIST